Her mouth travelled down his neck, scattering kisses at random, and his throat moved convulsively as he swallowed down his next words.

There was no point telling her that he wanted her feelings to last for longer than just this moment. It would only spoil what they had and he wouldn't do that.

He pulled her down onto his lap and kissed her with every scrap of pent-up emotion he possessed. They had barely three days to make a lifetime of memories and he wasn't going to waste a second. Maybe they would go back to normal after that, but maybe, just maybe, she would think about what had happened this weekend and wonder if she was right to be so against them having a real relationship.

It was the dimmest ray of hope, but it was something to hold onto.

D1638671

PRACTISING AND PREGNANT

**Dedicated doctors, determinedly single—
and unexpectedly pregnant.**

These dedicated doctors have one goal in life—to heal
patients and save lives. They've little time for love, but
somehow it finds them. When they're faced with single
parenthood too how do they juggle the demands and
dilemmas of their professional and private lives?

PRACTISING AND PREGNANT
Emotionally entangled stories of doctors in love
from Mills & Boon® Medical Romance™

THE PREGNANT SURGEON

BY
JENNIFER TAYLOR

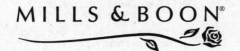

First published in Great Britain 2003
Harlequin Mills & Boon Limited,
Eton House, 18-24 Paradise Road, Richmond, Surrey TW9 1SR

© Jennifer Taylor 2003

ISBN 0 263 83873 0

Set in Times Roman 10½ on 12 pt.
03-0104-50690

Printed and bound in Spain
by Litografia Rosés, S.A., Barcelona

CHAPTER ONE

IT WAS her forty-second birthday today.

As she got out of her car, Joanna Martin felt suddenly depressed by the thought. It was odd because birthdays had never worried her before. With each year that had passed she had gained greater professional standing and that was all that had mattered to her. Even in these enlightened times there was still a great deal of opposition to women becoming surgeons. She'd had to work twice as hard as any man to achieve her goal, *and* she'd had to sacrifice an awful lot along the way.

Joanna frowned as she strode towards the hospital's main entrance. She had never considered her decision to focus on her career as a sacrifice before and it surprised her that the thought should have crossed her mind at this stage. Her recent promotion to head of surgery at St Leonard's Hospital in central London should have been all the proof she needed that she'd made the right decision. So maybe she'd had to forfeit any kind of a personal life but surely it had been worth it? She only had to recall the statistics to know how few women ever reached her level. Surgery was notoriously chauvinistic and very few women possessed the drive to make their way to the top.

She had done so, though, and she should be celebrating her achievements rather than feeling depressed by the thought of what she had given up along the way. Any woman could have a home and a family if that was what she wanted but not many had the kind of fulfilling career she enjoyed.

The thought was heartening and Joanna felt much better as she made her way along the maze of corridors to the lift. St Leonard's was one of the city's oldest hospitals and an absolute warren of rooms and passageways. Although there were signs posted at various strategic points, many people got lost on their way to the surgical department.

Joanna checked her watch as she got into the lift, wondering if she should ask her secretary to phone Reception and request that someone should show Dr Archer the way when he arrived. She had a full list that morning and the last thing she needed was her new senior registrar getting lost *en route*. It wouldn't be the first time it had happened although, to be fair, Dylan Archer hadn't struck her as someone who would need help finding his way. He'd seemed far too confident for that.

A shiver raced down Joanna's spine and she paused before opening the door to her office, wondering why she experienced this odd tingling sensation whenever she thought about the new registrar. She'd become aware of it at Dr Archer's interview but had put it down to the fact that she'd been anxious that they should appoint the right candidate to the post. St Leonard's had gone through a bad period a year or so ago when bad management, combined with a lack of funding, had taken its toll. However, the surgical team had been gradually rebuilding its reputation under her leadership and she'd been determined that her hard work wouldn't be ruined by appointing the wrong person to the post.

It had seemed a logical explanation at the time and

she'd thought no more about it until it had happened again when she had spoken to Dr Archer on the telephone the previous day. The minute she'd heard his deep voice coming over the line she'd experienced that same fluttering of her nerves, the same tightness in her stomach. She'd been so surprised that it had been difficult to concentrate as she'd explained to Dr Archer that she would be monitoring his work for the first week or so. It had been a relief when her beeper had gone off and she'd been able to excuse herself but she couldn't deny that it was worrying that she had found it happening again that day.

What *was* it about Dr Dylan Archer that disturbed her so much?

Joanna's mobile mouth thinned when she realised how foolish it was to waste time worrying about something so trivial. Opening the office door, she briskly greeted her secretary. 'Good morning, Lisa.'

'Morning, Ms Martin. The post is on your desk and Professor Humphrey's phoned to remind you about the dinner tonight.' Lisa handed her a yellow message slip. 'He said to tell you that twenty minutes should be long enough for your talk.'

'Right, that's fine.' Joanna barely glanced at the message as she headed towards her room, not needing any reminders about the coming evening. She had been asked to give a speech at the Royal College of Surgeons Annual dinner that night and had spent hours working on her script. It was an honour to be asked to speak at such a prestigious event but she wasn't nervous about it. She was extremely good at her job and she knew it—that gave her all the confidence she needed.

Thinking about confidence reminded her of Dr

Archer and she paused, trying to quell that irritating little flutter which had started up once more. 'Before I forget, Lisa, can you phone Reception and ask them to keep an eye open for Dr Archer? I have a very full list this morning and I don't want him getting lost when he's supposed to be assisting me. Perhaps one of the reception staff could fetch him up here?'

'Oh, he's already here, Ms Martin! He arrived about half an hour ago, in fact.' Lisa grimaced. 'Sorry. I should have told you that before, shouldn't I?'

'Yes, you should,' Joanna agreed, stifling a sigh. Lisa had been working for her for little more than a month and still tended to be rather scatterbrained at times. However, she was a hard worker so Joanna was prepared to allow her some leeway while she settled in. 'Anyway, you've told me now so it isn't a problem. Can you make some coffee, please, and bring it through to my room? Then you can print out this morning's list so I can run through it with Dr Archer before we go down to Theatre.'

'Oh, but he's already there—in Theatre, I mean. He asked me to tell you that's where he'd be if you wanted him.'

'In Theatre? What do you mean that he's *in Theatre*?' It was impossible to hide her annoyance and Joanna saw the young secretary look anxiously at her.

'A and E phoned to ask you to see a patient who'd been brought in. Dylan...I mean, Dr Archer was here at the time and he offered to go instead because you hadn't arrived.' Lisa sounded flustered as she tried to explain what had happened. 'Evidently, the man needed surgery urgently so Dr Archer took him to Theatre.'

'I see. Thank you, Lisa. In that case you may as

well forget the coffee for now. I'll go down to Theatre and see if Dr Archer needs a hand.'

Joanna summoned a smile before she went into her office but she couldn't deny that she was furiously angry. The fact that Dr Archer had taken it upon himself to operate after she had expressly told him that she wanted to monitor his work was bad enough. However, hearing her secretary refer to the registrar by his first name just seemed to make matters worse, though she couldn't understand why it should have annoyed her so much.

Although she preferred the junior staff to address her as Ms Martin, what business was it of hers if Dr Archer liked to be known by his first name? A lot of surgeons had dispensed with formality and Dylan Archer was obviously one of them. Nevertheless, Joanna couldn't help feeling irritated by the thought that her new registrar had made his presence felt so quickly. He'd been in the hospital for less than an hour and already her secretary was calling him Dylan and passing on messages for him!

Joanna's grey eyes darkened as she clipped her beeper to the waistband of her tailored black skirt. She wasn't used to her staff deliberately flouting her orders and wasn't prepared to put up with it from the newest member of her team. Smoothing the collar of her white silk blouse over the lapels of her suit jacket, she left her office and made her way to the stairs. The theatres were on the floor below and it wasn't worth waiting for the lift. The sooner she made it clear to Dr Archer that she expected him to toe the line the happier everyone would be.

Elective surgery had already started that day but Joanna bypassed Theatres one and two where members of her team were hard at work. She was confident that she could leave them to deal with their patients because she had spent hours supervising their training. It was the surgeon who was operating in Theatre three she needed to check on. Although Dr Archer's references had been excellent, she wanted to see for herself if he really was as good as his previous employers had claimed. It was an unwritten rule that everyone who joined her department should undergo a period of supervision, but Dr Archer obviously considered himself to be above that. However, there was no way that Joanna was prepared to compromise for anyone.

Just for a moment she found herself wondering if she might be overreacting before she dismissed the thought. This had nothing whatsoever to do with her *personal* feelings towards Dylan Archer. She hardly knew the man so how could she have any feelings about him of a personal nature? No, this was a strictly professional matter and she would make sure that he understood that.

She strode into the changing room and stripped off her suit jacket. She would scrub up and observe Dr Archer while he worked. And if there was the slightest doubt in her mind that he wasn't equal to the job, she would terminate his contract immediately.

'It's a real mess in here. The sooner we get this spleen out, the happier I'll be.' Dylan nodded his thanks as Lucy Porter, the sister in charge of Theatre three that day, swabbed away the blood that was leaking from the damaged organ.

The patient was a young man in his twenties who had been found unconscious in the street. He'd been beaten up and probably robbed as well because he'd had no money or any means of identification on him when he'd been found. The police were currently trying to find out who he was but the patient's identity was the least of Dylan's problems. His main concern was to make sure the young man didn't die from his injuries, and it was going to be a very close call from the look of him.

He deftly began clamping and severing the blood vessels leading to and from the spleen in readiness to removing it. The organ was badly damaged and it was difficult to see what he was doing because of the amount of blood. Lucy swabbed once more and once again Dylan nodded his thanks.

He'd been impressed by the whole team's professionalism from the minute they had entered Theatre. There had been none of the usual awkwardness that often arose when working with a new group of people. Everyone knew what he or she should be doing and got on with it, although he really wouldn't have expected anything else. He couldn't imagine Joanna Martin settling for second best where work was concerned.

Dylan's heart squeezed in an extra beat as an image of the beautiful head of surgery sprang to mind and he cursed under his breath. He wished it wouldn't keep doing *that*! The last time he'd reacted this way had been in his teens when he'd had a crush on his chemistry teacher. Every time the woman had entered the classroom, his heart had run riot. Maybe there'd been an excuse for such pathetic behaviour at seventeen but he was thirty-five years of age and he should be well past that stage by now, yet he couldn't seem to stop it happening. Every time he thought about Joanna Martin—and he seemed to think about her rather a lot—then wham, bang and his heart set off again. It was extremely worrying because the last thing he'd anticipated when he'd applied for this job had been that he would develop a crush on his boss!

Dylan's green eyes were wry as he applied himself to the task at hand. Fortunately, he'd performed this same operation a number of times before so there was little danger of him making a hash of it by letting his mind wander for the odd moment. He deftly clamped and snipped until he was ready to remove the organ, quickly depositing it in the dish Lucy offered him.

'Thanks.' Bending over the table again, he rinsed out the cavity then checked for any further soft tissue damage. He heard the soft whoosh as the doors into Theatre opened but didn't look up. He wanted to be absolutely sure that everything was fine before he started to close up…

The skin on the back of Dylan's neck suddenly began to prickle and his hands stilled. He knew that someone was standing behind him and had to fight the urge to turn round because he also knew who he would see. His heart suddenly seemed to fit in three beats where one would have been ample and he groaned in dismay. Hell and damnation! Surely he wasn't about to go to pieces because Joanna Martin was standing behind him and watching what he was doing with those sexy grey eyes?

'Is there a problem, Dr Archer?'

Her voice was as just cool as her expression had been throughout his interview so Dylan couldn't blame that for the rush of heat which invaded his body. He couldn't even blame her for the fact that she'd felt it necessary to check up on him even though it rankled just a little. In her shoes, he probably would have done the same thing—made sure the newcomer was up to the job. No, he only had himself to blame for the way he felt at that moment and he was willing, if not exactly eager, to admit it.

Joanna Martin had affected him in the strangest of ways from the moment he'd seen her in the interview room. She'd been wearing a tailored grey suit that day and as he had shaken her hand, he'd realised that the colour had exactly matched the colour of her eyes. It had been such a crazily irrelevant thought in the circumstances that it had been difficult to concentrate while the rest of the panel had introduced themselves. His gaze had kept returning to the woman sitting in the middle of the group as he'd taken stock of all sorts of other inconsequential details, like how velvety-soft her skin had looked and how her honey-blonde hair had seemed to shimmer as though sprinkled with stardust when it had caught the light from the chandelier…

'Dr Archer?'

Dylan exhaled sharply when Joanna Martin tersely reminded him that she was waiting for an answer. He saw Lucy glance at him curiously and felt a wash of colour run up his face. Fortunately the mask spared him from the embarrassment of having everyone notice his reaction, but *he* knew what had happened and it worried him. A lot. Making a fool of himself for any reason wasn't something he was in the habit of doing.

'Everything is fine, Ms Martin. Thank you.'

His tone was just as cool as Joanna's had been and he relaxed when he realised he had himself under control once more. He carried on with what he'd been doing—carefully checking that each of the blood vessels he'd needed to sever was firmly tied off. Even though the procedure wasn't a difficult one, he prided himself on always doing a good job and today it seemed more important than ever that he should be on his mettle when Joanna Martin was watching. He didn't intend to give her an opportunity to find fault with his work.

Now where had that idea sprung from?

Dylan had no idea why the thought should have popped into his head but all of a sudden he knew as surely as God made little green apples that Joanna Martin *wanted* to find fault with him. A frown crossed his handsome face as he deftly closed the incision in the patient's upper left abdomen because it didn't make sense.

'I see you decided to use a horizontal incision rather than a vertical one to remove the spleen, Dr Archer. What reason did you have for making that choice?'

Dylan's hands didn't falter even if his heart did when Joanna shot the question at him. Whereas before it had fitted in an extra beat now it seemed to have missed a couple. He gritted his teeth as he tried to control his annoyance at having his expertise called into question. If Ms Martin had any doubts about his capabilities she should have voiced them at his interview. That way he could have saved them both a great deal of inconvenience by not accepting the job as her registrar.

'Experience.'

His tone was clipped as he bit out the answer and he saw Lucy look at him again although there was a hint of sympathy in her eyes this time. Did Joanna Martin make a habit of interrogating her staff like this, perhaps? he wondered. Maybe she was some kind of a control freak and hadn't singled him out for special treatment but always behaved this way with a new member of the team?

The thought should have been reassuring but for some reason Dylan found it depressing to realise that Joanna might be treating him the same as everyone else. Even though he resented her interference he preferred to think that she viewed him as more than just one of the crowd.

The sheer stupidity of that thought made him laugh out loud and he had to hastily turn it into a cough because he really didn't want to have to explain what was so amusing. He finished closing up then glanced at Tom Barnes, the anaesthetist, relieved that the operation was over. Never had such a routine piece of surgery turned out to be so stressful.

'That's it, then. How's he doing?'

'Better than when he came in,' Tom replied laconically. He was a positive giant of a man with a mop of blond hair crammed under his Theatre hat. He'd been in the changing room when Dylan had arrived and had introduced himself, which had been a good job because otherwise Dylan would never have believed he was a *bona fide* medico.

Dressed in combat trousers and a tatty T-shirt bearing a surfing motif across its front, Tom hadn't looked like anyone's idea of a doctor. However, the minute they had stepped into Theatre Dylan had realised that Tom knew exactly what he was doing, which was probably why Joanna accepted him as part of her team. She was prepared to overlook Tom's appalling dress sense if it meant she had the calibre of staff she wanted working for her.

For some reason that thought didn't gel with the

image he'd been building up of Joanna Martin. As Dylan thanked the staff and left Theatre, he found himself wondering about a woman who dressed as conservatively as Joanna did and yet who was prepared to overlook such obvious quirks in those who worked for her. It simply didn't add up to someone who needed to be in control all the time and that naturally made him wonder why she'd been so keen to check up on him...

Unless she had been as eager to see him as he'd been to see her, of course. He could lie to himself until the grass turned blue but the reason why he'd arrived for work so early that morning had been because he had been longing to see Joanna again.

Dylan groaned as he dragged off his Theatre hat and raked an impatient hand through his black hair. He had to stop this nonsense before he made a complete ass of himself. He'd spoken to Joanna Martin for what? An hour, maybe a little more if he counted that conversation they'd had on the phone yesterday. And yet he was behaving as though—as though they were on the brink of having an *affair*!

Joanna Martin was his boss. Period. He had to get that fact into his head once and for all. However, when the door opened and he saw her coming out of Theatre he knew it wasn't going to be easy to think of her purely as that.

His vision suddenly blurred so that it seemed as though the room was lit by the glow of a million stars rather than by the glare from a neon striplight. Maybe it *was* crazy, and maybe *he* was crazy for thinking it, but he knew in his heart that the woman standing in front of him was going to mean a lot more to him than just someone he worked with. He might not like the idea and was sure that Joanna would hate it if she had any inkling of what he was thinking, but there was no way he could pretend about something so important.

Joanna Martin was the woman he was destined to fall in love with.

CHAPTER TWO

'I THINK we need to have a word, Dr Archer. If you would come to my office....'

'I'm sorry.'

Joanna jumped when Dylan interrupted her. He smiled but his green eyes were full of something which made her skin suddenly start to prickle. Why was he looking at her as though he'd never really seen her before? She had no idea but it was hard to hide her alarm when he continued.

'Obviously I've upset you and I apologise. It's the last thing I wanted to happen on my first day.'

Joanna cleared her throat, praying that he couldn't tell how off balance she felt. She wasn't sure what was going on but something was definitely wrong. Just for a second she found herself wondering if it was the fact that Dylan Archer was such a handsome man that had upset her equilibrium before she dismissed the idea. Dr Archer was a member of her staff, not a would-be suitor, and his looks had no bearing whatsoever on the situation.

'I am not upset, Dr Archer, I assure you,' she said firmly. 'However, it's obvious there are a few points we need to discuss—'

'Like me waltzing off to Theatre with a patient before you could check me out?'

Once again he cut in before she could finish and Joanna's mouth thinned. She'd spent too many years fighting her corner whilst various male colleagues had tried to talk above her to let a new *junior* colleague get away with such tactics.

'Perhaps you will do me the courtesy of letting me finish what I'm saying before you interrupt me again,' she suggested coldly, then broke off when Tom and Lucy came out of Theatre, pushing the patient on a trolley. She saw them glance at her and Dylan before they hurriedly carried on to the recovery bay, but it was obvious even from that brief look that they'd sensed that something was going on. A little colour touched Joanna's cheeks when it struck her once again that she might be making too big an issue out of this situation but she had to sort it out to her own satisfaction. *She* was in charge of this department and she wouldn't rest until she was sure that Dylan Archer understood that.

She turned to him again, struggling to keep her tone as neutral as possible. 'I'll see you in my office as soon as you've changed, Dr Archer.'

He didn't say anything this time although whether it was because he had decided to heed her advice, she wasn't sure. Joanna hurried to the women's changing room and quickly showered then dressed again. She checked her watch as she opened the door and sighed when she saw that she was already way behind schedule. She'd hoped to get an early start on the day's list but it would have to wait until she'd cleared up this misunderstanding. From what she had seen so far, Dr Archer appeared to be perfectly competent at his job, but she needed to be sure that he wasn't going to disrupt the workings of the whole team.

Joanna went back to her office and told Lisa to send Dr Archer in as soon as he arrived. She sat down at her desk, wanting to look suitably composed when he appeared. She frowned because she'd never had any difficulty taking charge of her staff before so why did it seem so important all of a sudden that she make the right impression?

She got up again and went to the mirror, tucking a loose strand of honey-gold hair into the heavy coil at the nape of her neck then running a finger over her eyebrows to smooth the tiny golden hairs into place. She never wore make-up when she would be operating and with her fair complexion tended to look rather washed-out in consequence. Maybe a holiday in the sun this year would give her a bit of much-needed colour?

'Lisa said to come straight in. I hope that's all right?'

Joanna swung round at the sound of that familiar, deep voice. She was a little embarrassed at being caught staring into the mirror but less so than she might have been if she hadn't had a more pressing concern to deal with. Bearing in mind that she'd spoken to Dylan Archer no more than half a dozen times to date, how had the timbre of his voice managed to imprint itself so clearly on her memory?

Frankly, Joanna had no idea how to explain such a strange phenomenon so decided to ignore it and concentrate instead on the reason why she'd asked Dr Archer to come to her office. She sat down behind her desk once more and waved him towards a chair.

'Please, sit down, Dr Archer. I shall be brief because we have a lot to get through today. I would have preferred it if you had waited until I'd arrived before you operated on that patient. As I explained to you yesterday on the phone, every new member of this team goes through a period of supervision. That rule applies to everyone who works here and there are no exceptions.'

'Then I can only apologise once again, Ms Martin. I assure you that I wasn't trying to flout your rules even though it may have appeared that way.'

His tone was nothing less than polite so Joanna had no idea why it should have set her teeth on edge. It was an effort not to snap back with some sharp retort but she knew it would be a mistake to do that. She had to remain in control at all times when dealing with Dylan Archer. Something told her it was the only way to handle the situation.

'I accept your apology, Dr Archer. Now that you've assured me it won't happen again we'll let the matter drop.'

'I'm sorry but I'm afraid I can't give you any such assurance, Ms Martin.'

Once again his tone was faultlessly polite. However, Joanna had heard the steely note it held and her brows rose steeply. 'I beg your pardon?'

'If we are to avoid any future misunderstandings I think it's only fair that I make my position clear, Ms Martin. Given the same set of circumstances, I would follow exactly the same course of action.'

His voice was even softer this time, soft and oddly dangerous-sounding. Joanna shivered when she heard the warning note it held. It was an effort to reply when she could feel the tremors working their way through her body.

'Would you care to elaborate, Dr Archer?'

'Certainly. If I had waited for you to arrive to supervise me then the patient could have died. I made my decision to go ahead and operate based on the experience I've gained over the last few years, and I believe it was the right decision, too.' He shrugged, his broad shoulders rising and falling beneath his suit jacket. 'Rules are all well and good, Ms Martin, but I will never endanger a patient's life by blindly sticking to them. I'm a qualified surgeon, not a student, and I hope that *you* will pay *me* the courtesy of remembering that.'

Joanna was completely floored and had no idea what to say. She knew she would be within her rights to reprimand him for speaking to her like that, but she was also aware that she'd handled the situation very badly. Dylan Archer *was* a highly skilled surgeon, which was the reason she'd been so keen to have him on her team, and if she'd been in his shoes, most probably she would have done the same thing. The patient could have died if the operation had been delayed so how could she honestly object to what he'd done? Why should she even want to when the outcome had been so satisfactory?

Her breath caught because there was another question that needed answering, one which was suddenly more important than all the rest: was she *really* acting out of professional concern or because of the way Dylan Archer made her feel as a woman rather than a surgeon?

Dylan forced himself to appear relaxed but it wasn't easy. He was used to making decisions and not having them questioned, yet Joanna Martin seemed set on treating him like the new kid on the block! He couldn't help wondering if he'd made a mistake by accepting the job at St Leonard's. He'd been happy enough in his last post, but he'd needed to broaden his experience, which was why he had applied for the job.

It was a well-known fact that Joanna Martin had worked wonders since she'd been appointed as head of surgery at St Leonard's and Dylan had honestly believed he could learn a lot from working with her. However, he was rapidly having second thoughts. His life was going to be hell if she continually took him to task over everything he did.

Maybe she got a kick out of throwing her weight around, he mused, before he dismissed the idea. Quite frankly, she didn't look any happier than he felt as she sat there behind her desk, her beautiful face set and her eyes so dark that he could see his own reflection in them.

Dylan's stomach muscles suddenly knotted at the sheer intimacy of that thought and he sucked in a calming lungful of air, wishing that he'd thought everything through properly before he'd come charging up to her office. With the benefit of hindsight he could see now that he'd needed more time to get himself together before he had faced Joanna after that earlier revelation. Frankly, it was no wonder that everything was going pear-shaped. How, in the name of heaven, could he have *known* that he'd met the woman he was destined to fall in love with?

Frankly, it defied all logic, or at least the bit of logic he could still dredge up. All he could do now was to try and salvage something from this mess.

'I'm sorry. I was way out of order for saying that, Ms Martin. I understand that you have a duty to the patients in this hospital and need to ensure that everyone receives the best possible care.'

'I do, but equally I'm one of the people who interviewed you for this post, Dr Archer. If I'd had any concerns about your suitability I should have raised them then.'

She shrugged and Dylan felt a wave of tenderness wash over him when he saw how confused she looked. He wanted to reach across the desk and squeeze her hand, reassure her that he wasn't offended—well, not now that she'd apologised, anyway—only he sensed it would be a mistake to do that. Joanna would just retreat back into her shell and then he'd have an even harder job eliciting a response from her.

Heat flashed through him when it struck him that the response he wanted from her wasn't solely a professional one. Maybe he *did* want her to treat him as the skilled surgeon he knew himself to be, but it wasn't his *only* attribute, as he would be happy to make clear. It was a relief when Joanna suddenly stood up because it effectively put an end to such crazy thoughts.

'I think it's time we got down to some work, don't you? We have a full list this morning, mainly minor elective surgery, although there is one case which you should find interesting.'

She headed for the door then glanced back when he followed her. Dylan felt his heart lift when she suddenly smiled at him. 'It should definitely give you a chance to show off your skills.'

'Sounds intriguing.'

He followed her out of the room, trying to control the thundering of his heart as they walked to the stairs together. Just because Joanna had smiled at him, it wasn't any reason to get too excited, he admonished himself, but sadly the advice seemed to fall on deaf ears. It was difficult to concentrate as she outlined the case for his benefit but he didn't intend to give her any reason to fault his work. He was good at what he did and he was going to prove it to her and the rest of the team!

'The patient's name is Ada Harper and she is one hundred years old. She's remarkably fit for her age which is the reason why we have agreed to operate on her. According to our colleagues in the cardiovascular department, Ada has the heart and lungs of a fifty-year-old.'

'Amazing!' Dylan laughed as he pushed open the swing doors so that Joanna could pass through them ahead of him. He inhaled deeply when he caught the fragrance of her perfume as she passed him. His whole body began to tingle before he ruthlessly forced his mind back to work, but it was alarming to realise just how responsive he was to this woman. He'd had more than his share of girlfriends over the years but he couldn't recall a single one of them having the effect on him that Joanna seemed to have.

'Amazing is the right word.' Joanna waited for him to catch up before continuing. 'Ada is a wonderful old lady, full of fun and brimming with energy. She would put many people half her age to shame, in fact. Unfortunately, she has a hiatus hernia which has been making her life a misery of late. The muscle at the junction between the oesophagus and the stomach has been badly affected and she's been suffering from severe reflux of the stomach's contents.'

'Nasty,' Dylan observed sympathetically. 'Has it just caused severe heartburn or has there been oesophagitis as well?'

'The oesophagus has been badly inflamed for some time, plus there are increasing periods when Ada can't eat at all because the muscles have gone into spasm,'

Joanna explained. 'Her GP tried all the usual remedies—a bland diet, eating several small meals each day instead of large ones—but the situation has got steadily worse. The GP referred Ada to a specialist at her local hospital and he agreed that the best treatment would be an operation to repair the hiatus hernia, but he refused to put her on his list, which is why she has ended up here.'

'That's rather unusual, isn't it?' he queried. 'If her local hospital refused to operate why did you agree to treat her?'

'Because one of the things I feel most strongly about is that age shouldn't prevent a person from receiving treatment. Ada is remarkably healthy apart from this problem and it isn't fair that her quality of life should be ruined because she's considered too old by some surgeons to undergo an operation.'

'I agree. It's one of the things that really angers me, too. If a person will benefit from surgery then it should be available to them.' He sighed because he'd had an uphill struggle in his last post, putting across that view. 'I'm afraid it usually comes down to economics. Many surgeons refuse to, quote, ''waste good money operating on someone who won't live long enough to appreciate it''.'

'Exactly! It's an attitude I abhor. Every case should be decided on its own merits and age should never be the deciding factor,' she agreed, smiling at him.

'Seems we're in accord on that, at least,' he said softly, his heart going into raptures when he saw the approval in her beautiful grey eyes.

'So it appears.' She briskly turned and hurried towards the female changing room but not before Dylan had seen the wash of soft rose colour that had tinted her cheeks. 'I'll see you in Theatre, Dr Archer,' she told him, without looking back.

'Of course.'

Dylan took a deep breath as the changing-room door shut behind her then let it out very, very slowly. It didn't help but, then, he hadn't honestly expected that it would. It would take more than a deep breath to cure this affliction.

He went into the men's changing room and stripped off his clothes then slid on a cotton scrub suit. The cotton felt cool against his skin, cool and soft, and he groaned because it made him think about Joanna and how her skin would feel. It would be cool and soft as well but, unlike the cotton, it would also be velvety smooth.

How he longed to touch her, ached to let his fingers explore her body, and the sheer depth of his desire shocked him because it was way out of proportion to the stage they were at in their relationship. They were two new—*very new*—colleagues, finding their feet as they worked together, and yet here he was lusting after her like a lover! What the hell was wrong with him? Was he having some kind of a mid-life crisis? Was it possible to have one at his age or did age make absolutely no difference in this situation as it shouldn't in so many others? He wanted Joanna Martin. He wanted her more than he'd believed it possible to want a woman, and it would have made no difference if he'd been ninety-five instead of thirty-five because he'd still have felt the same!

There, he'd admitted it, and it didn't make him feel any better. In fact, it made him feel like a total idiot. Joanna wasn't the least bit interested in him. He'd bet his last pound that she wasn't standing in the other changing room, lusting after him.

The thought brought him down to earth with a thump. Maybe he did want Joanna but he wouldn't do himself any favours by letting her know that.

Joanna slid her feet into a pair of backless Theatre clogs then went through to the scrub room. They were using Theatre three again and Lucy Porter was already in there, getting scrubbed up. She grinned when Joanna appeared.

'Hi! I was beginning to wonder what had happened to you. Problems with the new guy, by any chance? I had a feeling earlier that things might be getting a little tense between you two.'

'No, everything's fine. I just needed a word with Dr Archer, that's all. I'm sorry to have kept you waiting.'

Joanna went to the sink and quickly turned on the taps. Scooping a handful of antiseptic soap from the dispenser, she started lathering her arms. She felt rather uncomfortable about being asked a question like that. Normally, Lucy just wished her good day then carried on with what she was doing. She couldn't re-call the theatre sister passing a remark of a personal nature before and found herself wondering what had caused her to do so that day.

'No problem,' Lucy replied cheerfully, breaking open a sterile towel to dry her hands. 'It gave us time to have a cuppa before we set to again. With Dylan bringing up that emergency, we didn't get much chance to ease into the day. Poor old Tom looked very peaky from having to forgo his morning infusion of caffeine!'

'Then it all worked out for the best, didn't it?' Joanna replied rather lamely.

She took a nailbrush off the shelf and set to work with gusto, wondering why she was so uncomfortable about making conversation. She'd worked with Lucy for several years now yet this was the most they'd ever said to one another. Their previous conversations had been confined to work but, then, *most* conversations she had nowadays were work-related. When was the last time she'd exchanged a bit of idle gossip with anyone? It was faintly alarming to realise that she couldn't remember.

'Aha, so you've drawn the short straw and got the new guy again, Lucy.' Dylan came into the scrub room and Joanna swung round when she heard his voice. Just for a moment her gaze rested on his powerful frame before she hurriedly resumed what she'd been doing, but it was already too late because the sight of him had imprinted itself in her mind by then. The gushing water and frothing soap-suds suddenly blurred as his image swam before her eyes, and she gulped. That scrub suit had clung to *every* powerful line of his body, highlighting muscles that looked far too fit for someone who spent his working life bent over an operating table!

The picture sharpened and she had to draw in a ragged breath when a wave of dizziness assailed her. Were Dylan's legs really that long or was it just a trick of her imagination? And his shoulders—could they possibly be that broad without the benefit of padding? She knew she shouldn't look at him again but the urge to satisfy her curiosity was too strong to resist.

She glanced round, deliberately letting her gaze rest on his broad back because it seemed vital that she should answer those questions. He was reading through the patient's notes so she had ample time to take stock without him noticing and didn't waste a second as she began mentally listing his attributes. Well-shaped head, strong neck, broad shoulders, neat waist…

Her gaze suddenly came to his bottom and to her dismay refused to move on. She tried to make her eyes obey her but to no avail. Joanna bit her lip. There was something decidedly sinful about the idea of standing there, ogling Dylan Archer's taut derrière so perfectly displayed by the thin scrub-suit trousers.

He suddenly looked round and Joanna flushed when he caught her staring at him. A slow grin spread across his face and she had to bite back her groan of dismay. She had never felt so embarrassed in her life and there was absolutely nothing she could do to salvage her pride.

'Don't worry, Joanna. I know exactly what you're thinking.'

'You do?' she squeaked, her vocal cords knotting in mortification.

'Yes. And I promise you that I'm going to stick strictly to the rules from now on.' He waggled the folder of notes at her. 'I understand that you need to supervise me and it isn't a problem. Really. I can tell you're worried about how I'll react but there's no need.'

He suddenly frowned, his black brows drawing together over those gorgeous emerald green eyes. 'That *is* what's bothering you? You're worried that I'll take offence but I promise you that I don't mind if you spend the day peering over my shoulder.'

Maybe *he* didn't mind but *she* did!

All of a sudden Joanna knew that the last thing she needed was to spend the day monitoring what Dylan was doing. She could just imagine how stressful it would be to have to stand behind him in Theatre, staring at...

'No!' She cut off that train of thought because she didn't dare let it reach its natural conclusion. She had to stop thinking about Dylan's bottom!

'No?'

'No.' She heard the bewilderment in his voice and hurried on. She couldn't afford to let this situation get out of hand. She had to remember that she was forty-two years old and that getting involved with a junior colleague would be professional suicide. Maybe men could bend the rules to suit themselves but she couldn't take such a risk. She refused to let herself become the butt of a lot of puerile jokes and damaging gossip.

'I won't be monitoring your work, Dr Archer, because there is no need. I saw enough this morning to know that you are more than capable of working on your own.'

She elbowed the taps off and took the towel Lucy offered her, deliberately ignoring the shock on the other woman's face. Maybe it *was* unheard of her to compromise but sometimes a situation demanded a more flexible approach. Tossing the towel into the basket, she slid her hands into the latex gloves that Lucy offered her before glancing at Dylan again.

'We shall split the list between us. I'll be working in Theatre two if you need me.'

She briskly headed for the door and didn't pause when Dylan said softly behind her, 'Thank you.'

Joanna didn't reply because she didn't want to make

an issue out of her decision. She went straight to Theatre two and informed the staff that she would be operating in there that morning while Dr Archer, the new senior registrar, was working in Theatre three. The announcement caused a bit of a stir but she told herself that it was because they hadn't been expecting her and had nothing to do with the fact that she had seen fit to bend the rules for a newcomer.

Fortunately, everyone soon settled down and within a few minutes her first patient was being wheeled in. Joanna had a brief word with the young woman who'd been admitted for surgery on her hand. She was suffering from Dupuytren's contracture—a condition whereby tissues beneath the palm of the hand thickened and shortened, causing difficulty in straightening the fingers. Joanna planned to cut and separate the bands of tissue to free the woman's fingers. It was an operation she had performed before successfully so she assured the patient that everything would be fine then moved aside while the anaesthetist got on with his job.

It was a scene she'd witnessed too many times to count but all of a sudden it felt as though she was seeing it afresh. Her vision seemed sharper than it had been before, her hearing more acute, and she couldn't understand what had changed until it struck her that it was Dylan Archer's arrival which had made the difference. The scene she was witnessing seemed far more vivid than normal because of his presence, and the realisation scared her.

Her life had been going according to plan and she didn't want anything to change, but she might not be able to stop it. Dylan Archer's advent into her life had added a new dimension to the equation and, whether she liked the idea or not, she might not be able to get things back to how they had been before.

CHAPTER THREE

'GOOD work!'

Dylan smiled when Tom Barnes clapped him on the back as he came into the changing room. They had just finished their last operation for the day—the one to repair Ada Harper's hiatus hernia—and he knew that Tom was as pleased as he was that it had gone so well. Ada was now in Recovery and would be transferred to the surgical ward as soon as she came round from the aneasthetic. However, Dylan wasn't anticipating any problems.

'Thanks, but you should give yourself a pat on the back as well. Anaesthetising a patient of that age is no mean feat, buddy!'

'I know.' Tom's face split into a wide grin as he stripped off his Theatre greens and tossed them into the laundry hamper. 'I did one heck of a job in there, too, didn't I?'

Dylan gave a bark of laughter at such unashamed lack of modesty. 'You certainly did. It's no wonder Joanna overlooks your dodgy dress sense if that's any indication of your expertise.'

'What do you mean, "dodgy dress sense"?' Tom tried—and failed—to look suitably offended as he took his T-shirt off a peg and inspected it. 'This is the real McCoy, I'll have you know. A genuine, *bona fide* surfer's shirt, only given to those brave souls who've ridden the Big One.'

'The Big One, as in Hawaii?' Dylan whistled. 'Then

I stand in awe of your surfing talents as well as your anaesthetising skills. No wonder you're the star of Joanna's team.'

'Thank you kindly. It's nice to be appreciated although I might need to look to my laurels now you've joined us.' Tom dragged a towel out of his locker and flung it over his shoulder as they headed for the showers.

'What do you mean?' Dylan paused and looked at the other man in surprise.

'That my undoubted talents might not be enough to keep me in pole position as our revered boss's star performer.' Tom grinned as he reached a long arm into the cubicle and turned on the water. 'The lovely Joanna obviously has a soft spot for you.'

'I don't know what you mean,' Dylan denied, stepping into the cubicle and hurriedly turning on the jets. The water was icy cold and he gasped when it hit him. Shivering, he quickly adjusted the temperature then looked up when Tom's voice came from the neighbouring stall.

'It's unheard of for Joanna not to give a new recruit a thorough going over,' Tom shouted above the noise of the water. 'I can't recall her ever letting anyone get on with the job without first checking to ensure he knows what he's doing. You can have a list of references as long as your arm but she still has to be sure you're equal to the task, so how come she gave you free rein today? What's your secret?'

'Oh, I expect she'd seen enough when I operated on that chap with the ruptured spleen,' Dylan replied uncomfortably, because he'd heard the speculation in Tom's voice. A wave of heat that had little to do with the temperature of the water rushed through him and he grimaced. The thought that Joanna might have treated him as a special case was both intriguing and scary. Whilst he appreciated the fact that she trusted him enough to do his job, he didn't want to get carried away by the idea that she might have afforded him special treatment for any reason other than his professional skills…

The hell he didn't!

Did Joanna see him as rather *more* than just a very new colleague? he wondered euphorically. And was *that* why she'd waived her rules today? His mind ran riot with the idea so that he missed what Tom said and had to apologise. 'Sorry. What was that?'

'I said that it still isn't like her to be so lenient.' The water in the neighbouring stall was suddenly switched off but Tom didn't bother lowering his voice. It came booming over the partition.

'Joanna is paranoid about making sure everything is done to her exacting standards. That woman lives and breathes surgery to the exclusion of everything else. I don't know how you managed it, my friend, but you've achieved the impossible. You've made Joanna Martin behave like a human being for once, and I and the rest of the staff salute you!'

Joanna left the changing room as soon as she was dressed. It had been a busy day but she was pleased with what she had achieved. She checked her watch as she hurried towards the stairs and smiled when she realised that she'd have time to go over her speech before she needed to get ready for the dinner. She'd got through her list that day in record time thanks to the fact that Dylan Archer had taken half her patients, so she may as well make the most of the early finish.

Although she was confident that she had covered all the points she wanted to make, it wouldn't hurt to go through her notes one last time…

Joanna is paranoid about making sure everything is done to her exacting standards. That woman lives and breathes surgery to the exclusion of everything else. I don't know how you managed it, my friend, but you've achieved the impossible. You've made Joanna Martin behave like a human being for once, and I and the rest of the staff salute you!

Joanna was passing the men's changing room when Tom's voice suddenly boomed out into the corridor. She came to an abrupt halt, feeling herself trembling when she realised what he'd said. Did the staff really consider her dedication as a form of paranoia? Might it even be true? She didn't want to believe it but she couldn't deny there was some truth in what Tom had said. She *did* live and breathe surgery but she'd needed to be completely focused to get where she was. She was a woman in a man's world and it had needed total commitment to get her this far…

But surely she was entitled to a life apart from her work?

The thought slid into her mind and she frowned because it was the second time that day she'd found herself questioning the life she had chosen. It didn't make sense because she was perfectly happy with what she had achieved, but then the rest of Tom's statement didn't make much sense either. To suggest that Dylan Archer possessed any kind of power over her was ludicrous!

Joanna's lips snapped shut as she hurried to the stairs. She deliberately closed her mind to the little voice inside her head which was calmly pointing out that the suggestion had simply mirrored her earlier thoughts. Maybe she *had* toyed with the idea that Dylan Archer seemed to have a strange effect on her, but a stint in Theatre had soon brought her feet safely back onto the ground. Dr Archer was a colleague and that was all he would ever be. The chances of him turning her 'into a human being'—whatever that meant—were nonexistent. She didn't intend to get that involved with him!

Joanna was more than a little irked by the suggestion as she let herself into her office. Fortunately, it was gone five and Lisa had left so she was spared having to make small-talk with her secretary. She found her speech then sat down at her desk. There was a stack of letters in her tray for signing but she would deal with them after she had read through her speech. She wanted to be sure she was word perfect because it was important that she should put on a good show that night. She was Joanna Martin, Fellow of the Royal College of Surgeons, Head of Surgery at St Leonard's Hospital, and that was something to be proud of. Whether or not her staff considered her to be paranoid or *inhuman* was neither here nor there.

Joann quickly read through the speech from start to finish but the words which had sounded so fluent and interesting that morning now sounded stilted and pompous. Panic hit her as she pictured herself standing up in front of the august gathering and watching them yawning with boredom. What on earth was she going to do? She couldn't possibly hope to rewrite the whole speech at this late stage.

'Sorry to bother you, Joanna, but I just wanted to tell you that Ada Harper is fine… Joanna? Are you OK?'

Joanna looked up when she heard Dylan's voice. He was standing in the doorway to her office and the concern she could see on his handsome face suddenly made her want to cry.

'I'm fine,' she replied thickly, struggling to control herself. She couldn't recall the last time she'd felt this emotional and it was hard to hold back her tears now.

'Of course you're not fine! That's obvious so tell me what's wrong. Maybe I can do something to help?'

His tone was even gentler now, gentle and persuasive and so wonderfully tempting that she longed to unburden herself, but how could she? How could she show any sign of weakness when she was supposed to be in charge of this department? It could undermine her credibility to such an extent that she might find it impossible to do her job. Then she would have to hand in her notice and start afresh somewhere else although it wouldn't be easy because news travelled fast. It would be all round London that she hadn't been able to cope and then, of course, people would say it was her own fault for aiming so high in the first place…

'Hey, come on! Nothing can be that bad.'

She hadn't realised that Dylan had crossed the room and nearly shot ten feet into the air when she felt his arm go around her shoulders. He bent so that their faces were level and her heart stumbled to a halt when she saw the tenderness in his eyes.

No man should be *allowed* to look at a woman like that, she thought dazedly. It gave him an unfair advantage because it made it impossible for her to think rationally. When a man looked at a woman the way Dylan was looking at her she became putty in his hands.

Joanna shrugged off his arm and pushed back her

chair in one rapid movement that startled her as much as it startled him. She leapt to her feet and glared at him. 'I have no idea what you think you're doing, Dr Archer!'

'I'm trying to find out what's wrong and if I can help in any way. I thought that was obvious.'

His tone was clipped although the look on his face was so comical that Joanna experienced a sudden urge to laugh. Did he have any idea how stunned he looked at that moment? Of course not! He was the type of man who was normally in control of himself *and* the situation and it must be a rare event for him to find himself out of his depth like this.

The thought should have been comforting but for some reason it just served to knock her even further off balance. Joanna felt her insides quiver as she tried to deal with the thought that Dylan was as unsure about what was happening between them as she was. What had Tom said about Dylan making her behave like a human being? Well, it was true because he made her feel things that she'd never experienced before.

All of a sudden Joanna realised what dangerous ground she was on. She'd spent the whole of her adult life focusing on her work to such an extent that her emotional life had been neglected. Oh, she'd had the odd romantic liaison over the years but never anything serious. She hadn't been prepared to put in the time or the effort it had needed to maintain a relationship when she'd had her career to consider.

The men she'd dated had soon tired of coming second to her job so for the past few years she had refused any invitations. It had seemed pointless going out on a date when she wasn't interested in having a relationship with anyone, yet she realised with a sudden flash of insight that she would be interested if Dylan asked her out. The thought terrified her because she knew in her heart that there could be no compromises in that situation. It would be all or nothing if she got involved with a man like Dylan, and that was out of the question. She wasn't prepared to sacrifice her career for love.

Dylan walked over to the door then turned and walked all the way back to the desk just to prove to himself that he was capable of making his limbs obey him. He felt a little better after he'd done it, more able to cope with making his mind listen to reason. If Joanna didn't want his help then that was the end of the story.

Only it wouldn't be the end because he would be forced to spend the rest of the night worrying about her, wouldn't he?

He swore under his breath, wishing not for the first time that day that he'd never taken this wretched job. If he hadn't taken it he would be carrying on as normal. He glanced at his watch and made a few rapid calculations. He should be on his way home by now and trying to decide nothing more stressful than which restaurant he would take the current woman in his life to for dinner. Once dinner was over they might either go on to a club or back to his flat depending on the stage they were at in their relationship, although lately it had been rare that he'd invited anyone to spend the night with him.

Dylan frowned when it struck him just how long it had been, in fact, since he'd slept with a woman. It wasn't because of a lack of willing partners either, but he just wasn't interested in casual sex nowadays. He wanted more from a relationship than a few hours of physical pleasure, things like closeness and commitment, a sense of them belonging together. Casual sex was a bit like scratching an itch—good while it lasted but quickly forgotten afterwards—and he wanted more than that. In fact, when he asked Joanna to spend the night with him it would be because they *both* knew they were making a commitment to each other.

The thought astounded him. He swung round and marched back to the door again then stood there while he took half a dozen deep breaths to clear his head. Putting the horse before the cart wasn't in it! Commitment and Joanna Martin were two concepts which should never have been uttered in the same breath at this stage, so how come they had sneaked into his head?

He had no idea but what he did know was that he'd be in serious trouble if Joanna discovered what he'd been thinking. The last thing he could afford at this stage in his career was to be dismissed, yet it was a distinct possibility if she thought she was in danger of being compromised in any way.

Dylan called on all his resources before he turned to face her, and even then found his resolve wavering when he saw how upset she looked. He ached to comfort her but he forced himself to behave with decorum. Joanna was his boss and he was going to treat her as such even if it killed him—which it very well might!

'Look, Joanna, I'm not trying to pry but if there is any way I can help you only need to say the word.' He shrugged when she glanced up, hoping he looked suitably nonchalant. 'The offer's there but it's up to you whether or not you accept it.'

'I…um… Thank you. I appreciate your concern but everything is fine, I assure you.'

Dylan's nostrils flared with impatience when he heard the distance in her voice. She was deliberately trying to blank him and it hurt to be on the receiving end of such tactics. However, deep down he knew there would be little to gain but a lot to lose if he pursued the matter so he merely shrugged.

'Fine. In that case I'll say goodnight. Have a pleasant evening.'

'Fat chance of that!'

He'd already taken a couple of steps out of the door when he heard that comment and he stopped dead. He looked round, feeling his very bones melting with tenderness when he saw how appalled she looked. It was obvious that she hadn't intended to say that and it touched his heart that the words had spilled out despite her intentions. Maybe Joanna found it a bit more difficult to maintain her aura of cool professionalism in front of him than she did in front of the rest of her staff?

The thought was far too tantalising to ignore so Dylan didn't try. He slowly made his way back into the room. 'Want to explain that comment?' he asked, half expecting a rebuff. His heart lifted when she grimaced because it was the first time she'd *willingly* betrayed any sign of weakness in front of him.

'I have to give a speech at the Royal College of Surgeons annual dinner tonight and I've just realised that what I've written is a complete load of rubbish.' She tapped a fingernail on the neatly typed notes piled on her desk. 'It's flat, boring and will have everyone snoring before I reach the second paragraph!'

'Then it should be fine.' He grinned when she looked at him in surprise. 'Every single speech I've ever heard at the dinner has had me nodding off so yours should fit the occasion perfectly.'

There was total silence for a moment and he gritted his teeth as he wondered if his flippancy had offended her. This was obviously important to her and he shouldn't have tried to make light of her concerns. A little chuckle suddenly broke the silence and he heaved a sigh of relief when he realised she was laughing.

'Thank heavens for that! I thought I'd mortally offended you.'

'You didn't. Not at all.' She chuckled again, a throaty sound that made his toes curl and caused an immediate reaction in another part of his anatomy as well. Dylan shifted uncomfortably when he felt his body make its own appreciative statement as to how it felt about that alluring little laugh.

'You've made me see how stupid I'm being so thank you very much. I'd got myself so keyed up about making the perfect speech that I'd lost sight of the fact that most of the speeches I've listened to have bored me rigid.' She grinned as she briskly gathered up her notes. 'At least mine won't rock the boat and give anyone a heart attack by being too challenging!'

'I'm sure you're doing yourself an injustice,' he protested, desperate to get his mind back on the subject under discussion rather than what was currently occupying it. Thoughts like that—and he certainly wasn't going to elaborate on what sort of thoughts they were—were totally inappropriate.

'I doubt it but who cares? I shall do my best and just have to hope that it's enough.'

'Nobody can do more than that, Joanna. Nobody expects any more than that, in fact,' he gently pointed out. He sighed when she looked at him questioningly.

He really didn't want to start making more waves but he could hardly refuse to explain what he'd meant.

'You're far too hard on yourself. It isn't good to keep striving for perfection all the time.'

She laughed shortly. 'You hardly know me, Dr Archer, so I really can't see that you're qualified to make that kind of judgement.'

'Maybe I don't know you all that well but it's obvious that you are completely dedicated to your work,' he countered.

'And is that your opinion or are you quoting your esteemed colleague. What was it that Dr Barnes said? Ah, yes, that's it. I'm paranoid about making sure everyone works to my standards and that the staff all salute you for making me behave like a human being. I think I got it right, didn't I?'

Dylan's heart sank, not because Joanna had somehow overheard Tom's comments but because of the hurt in her voice. It had upset her to hear herself being spoken about in those less than flattering terms and he felt guilty about having been part of the conversation.

'Maybe Tom did say all that but he said it out of concern rather than because he was criticising you. I've only been here a day but it's obvious the esteem your team have for you, Joanna. You're a wonderful doctor, a superb surgeon and you are doing what any surgeon hopes to do—you are improving people's lives with your skill.'

Joanna felt a lump come to her throat because there was no doubt that Dylan meant every word. Maybe he had been trying to smooth over an awkward moment but that didn't detract from the fact that he believed what he had said.

She cleared her throat, not wanting him to see how touched she was by the compliment. 'Thank you. I appreciate your comments, Dr Archer.' She shrugged, suddenly wanting to lighten the mood because she wasn't sure she could handle so much emotion. 'I should have remembered the old adage about listeners never hearing anything good about themselves.'

'And Tom should have had the sense to lower his voice.' He grinned but his eyes were full of tenderness again and her heart surged because every time he looked at her she could see it in his eyes. 'He could waken the dead with a voice as loud as that. No wonder nobody dares die when he's in charge of their anaesthesia!'

Joanna burst out laughing. 'If only it were that simple! Still, I was pleased to hear that Ada Harper came through her op. She's such a game old lady and I was keeping my fingers crossed it would be all right.'

'She'll be fine. I'm going to pop down to see her in a few minutes.' He checked his watch and frowned. 'What time does the dinner start? These events usually kick off quite early so shouldn't you be on your way home to get changed?'

'I brought my clothes into work the other day,' she explained. 'I knew I had full list today and that I would need to spend extra time supervising...' She broke off, not wanting to remind him about her decision not to supervise him. She still wasn't completely comfortable with the fact that she had waived the rules for him.

Dylan grinned. 'Supervising me? That's what you were going to say, wasn't it?' He laughed when she nodded. 'Thought so, and may I say that I feel honoured that you let me loose on your patients without being subjected to a thorough check-up first.'

'I'd seen enough this morning to know you were up to the job,' she said shortly, not wanting to delve too deeply into the reason for her leniency. Dylan was an excellent surgeon and that was all that mattered.

'That's what I told Tom,' he agreed blandly but there was a twinkle in his eyes that sent a flood of heat rushing through her body.

'Good.' Joanna glanced at her watch because it was time she brought the conversation to an end. It wouldn't help to keep thinking about why she'd bent the rules for Dylan so she would put it out of her mind. 'Anyway, I'd better start getting ready.'

'And I'd better get down to the ward to see Mrs Harper.' Dylan went to the door then stopped. 'Best of luck with your speech tonight, not that you'll need it, of course.'

'Oh, of course not,' she agreed, pulling a face. 'I just wish I had your confidence when I have to stand up there in front of everyone.'

'I could always come to the dinner with you.'

'I'm sorry?' She looked at him in surprise.

'I have a ticket for tonight's little shindig sitting on my mantelpiece back home.' He shrugged. 'I was supposed to be attending the dinner to represent my old department at St Clemence's but decided not to go after I accepted the job here. I had been meaning to cancel my place but forgot about it with all the palaver of changing jobs. The ticket should still be valid, but even if it isn't I could always wait outside in the foyer and just slip in to listen to your speech.'

'You'd really do that for me?' she asked in amazement. 'Stand outside while we eat so you can listen to my speech?'

'Of course, if you want me to. Do you, Joanna? Would you like me to come with you tonight and cheer you on?'

CHAPTER FOUR

'LADIES and gentlemen, it is my great pleasure to introduce our next speaker this evening, Ms Joanna Martin.'

Polite applause rippled around the room as Joanna made her way to the podium. Placing her notes carefully on the stand, she glanced towards the back of the room and felt her heart lift when Dylan gave her a smile of encouragement. He had been waiting outside the hotel when she'd arrived that night, looking devastatingly handsome in his formal dinner suit. Joanna's heart had skipped several beats as he'd helped her out of the taxi. She'd felt a little self-conscious about her own appearance at first. However, the appreciation in his eyes as he'd taken stock of her black velvet cocktail dress had soon convinced her that she'd made the right choice.

Unfortunately, they hadn't been able to sit together because the table plans had been prepared many weeks earlier and couldn't be changed at such a late stage in the proceedings, but they'd had time for a drink in the bar before dinner had started and that had done a lot to settle her nerves. Now, as she stood in front of the audience, Joanna could feel Dylan willing her to make a success of her speech and the very last of her jitters faded away. She was going to do this and she was going to do it well because it was what Dylan expected of her!

'Ladies and gentlemen, esteemed colleagues, let me

begin with some background information for those of you who don't know me...'

Twenty minutes later Joanna stepped down from the podium to resounding applause. Her speech had gone down far better than she'd dared hope and several people congratulated her on her way back to her seat. There was one more speech after hers but she barely heard a word because she was on such a high. She stood up and shook hands with her table companions once the evening was brought to a conclusion then looked round to see if she could spot Dylan in the crowd. She wanted to hear his opinion before she would be completely satisfied.

'That was brilliant, Joanna, absolutely brilliant! What a performance.'

All of a sudden he was standing beside her and her heart swelled with delight when she heard the praise in his voice. 'You really think it went OK, then?'

'Yes! It couldn't have been better. And the proof of that was that I didn't hear a single snore throughout the whole time you were speaking.'

She burst out laughing. 'You idiot!'

'Idiot? Here I am, telling you the truth, and you accuse me of being an idiot. I'm absolutely gutted.'

He tried to look suitably wounded but the laughter in his green eyes completely ruined the effect. A surgeon from Guy's came over to speak to her at that moment so Joanna was forced to make conversation for a few minutes. She gracefully accepted the compliments that were showered on her but inside she was seething with impatience. She didn't want to waste time talking to anyone else when she could be talking to Dylan.

Her heart suddenly plummeted when she realised

how dangerous it was to think like that. Dylan had been kind enough to offer his support that evening but she mustn't make too much of it. He'd probably considered it his duty to accompany her because she was his boss.

The thought was so deflating that all the pleasure seemed to disappear from the evening. It was difficult to disguise her dismay as she said goodbye to the surgeon from Guy's and turned to Dylan again and she saw him frown.

'What's up, Doc?' he asked, the teasing note in his voice as he trotted out the phrase completely at odds with the concern in his eyes.

'Nothing. I'm fine, or I will be as soon as I get out of this scrum.'

She fixed a smile to her mouth as she made her way through the crowd that had gathered around the door. Several people tried to stop her *en route* to offer their congratulations, but Joanna fobbed them off with the excuse that she was on call and had to leave. They were all used to their social lives coming second to their work so they accepted what she said without question, but it was a relief when she finally reached the foyer. Now she just needed to fetch her coat and she could go home.

'I'll collect our coats then we can find a taxi.'

Joanna stopped when she realised that Dylan had followed her out. She knew that she must make it clear that she didn't expect him to leave because she was going home. 'There's no need...' she began, then realised she was speaking to thin air because he was already on his way to the cloakroom.

She sighed as she watched him crossing the foyer and wondered how she could explain that she didn't want to share a taxi with him without appearing rude. She would prefer to make her own way home and spare herself any possible awkwardness. She didn't want to find herself in the difficult position of having to invite Dylan into her flat.

A frown puckered her brow because there was no question of her asking Dylan into her flat even if he did accompany her home. Frankly, she couldn't understand why the thought should have occurred to her and was still pondering on it when he returned with her coat draped over his arm. He helped her on with it then looked enquiringly at her.

'Do you want to go straight home or can I persuade you to join me for a nightcap? There's a rather nice little bar just round the corner from here and we could have a drink there while you unwind after your star performance.'

'It's very kind of you to offer but I think it would be best if I went straight home. I'm second on call tonight so I can't have anything to drink. Don't let that stop you going, though.' She held out her hand, relieved to have found an excuse to bring the evening to a speedy conclusion. 'Thank you for coming with me tonight. I really appreciate it.'

'It was my pleasure.' He took her hand but instead of shaking it, as she'd expected him to do, he squeezed her fingers. 'And I think I'll give that drink a miss. It's no fun drinking on your own so I'll find us a taxi. Why don't you wait here? There's no point you standing outside in the cold.'

'I wouldn't dream of spoiling your evening,' she protested, her heart knocking painfully against her ribs. Maybe it was silly to make a fuss but the thought of Dylan accompanying her back to her flat made her feel very on edge. It would be rude not to invite him in for coffee after he had gone to so much trouble, but something told her that she could be playing with fire if she asked him into her home.

'And leave you to make your own way home?' He shook his head. 'No way. For one thing my mother would have my guts for garters if she found out. She's a stickler when it comes to good manners and drummed it into me that I should never, *ever* let a lady travel home on her own at night. You wouldn't want to get me into trouble, would you?'

'I…um…' Joanna began, completely flummoxed by the idea of Dylan being in trouble with his mother.

He grinned at her. 'Good! That's settled, then. I'll go and find us a taxi.'

He didn't waste any more time debating the issue as he hurried away. Joanna shook her head in disbelief. How had she ended up falling in with his plans when it had been the last thing she'd intended? She still hadn't worked it out by the time he came back to tell her the taxi was waiting outside, but she knew that she must be on her guard in future. Dylan Archer had a positive talent for getting his own way, it appeared.

It was an unsettling thought and Joanna found it hard to dismiss it as Dylan escorted her out to the cab. She got into the back then glanced round when she realised Dylan had said something to her. 'I'm sorry?'

'I was just asking where you live so I can tell the driver where to take us,' he explained.

'Oh, yes, of course.' She quickly told the cabby her address then slid along the seat when Dylan climbed in beside her. His thigh brushed hers as he made himself comfortable and Joanna bit her lip when she felt tiny pinpricks of heat prickling her skin. She stared out of the taxi's window as they set off but she was so conscious of Dylan sitting beside her that she didn't dare look at him in case he guessed how she felt. Frankly, she couldn't understand why he had this effect on her. She wasn't a complete innocent even though the few relationships she'd had hadn't lasted very long. However, she knew enough to state categorically that no man had made her feel the way Dylan did.

'I never get tired of the hustle and bustle of London, do you?'

She jumped when he spoke, feeling the vibrations from his deep voice strumming along her taut nerves. 'I've never really thought about it,' she murmured distractedly, trying to get a grip on herself.

'Then you must be a committed townie. You don't notice the downside of living in the city because you accept it as part and parcel of your life?'

He turned to look at her and Joanna felt her nerves tighten that bit more when she saw the curiosity in his eyes. Dylan *really* wanted to know how she felt about this issue. He wasn't just making conversation for the sake of it—he wanted to find out all about her. The thought made her feel both scared and elated, a potent combination when her emotions were so finely balanced.

'I love the city,' she admitted, knowing that she couldn't let him see how vulnerable she felt. It was as though the past twenty years had disappeared and all the confidence she'd gained during that time had melted away so that she was back to being a gauche teenager once more. A teenager who was out on her very first date as well!

'I certainly can't imagine living anywhere else,' she

hurried on, wanting to rid herself of that crazy notion. She *wasn't* a teenager and this *wasn't* a date, and the sooner she got those facts straight in her head the better it would be. 'Oh, I'll admit that I enjoy spending time in the country but I like the convenience of city living too much to ever consider relocating.'

'How about if you had a family? City life isn't exactly conducive to raising children so maybe you'd change your mind then?'

'There's not much chance of that happening.'

'You mean that you wouldn't change your mind, or that you can't see yourself ever having a family?'

Joanna frowned when she heard the husky note in his voice. She felt her heart race when she saw the expression on his face. There was no doubt that her answer was important to him, but why? She didn't understand. Why should it matter so much to Dylan how she felt about having a family?

Dylan realised he was holding his breath as he waited for Joanna to say something. He made himself breathe out then in but it didn't alter the fact that her answer really mattered to him. That he would have a family at some stage in his life had always been a foregone conclusion. He'd never had to think about it because he loved kids and knew that he wanted some of his own one day. There had never been any sense of urgency about having them because he'd also known that he needed to find the right woman first. Was Joanna that woman?

The thought caught him completely unawares and he gasped. He saw Joanna frown as she leant across the seat and thumped him on the back. 'Are you all right?'

'Fine. Just a bit of tickle in my throat.' He managed to suck in a little air, enough to stop the wheezing, and dredged up a smile. 'That's better now.'

'Good.' She sat back in her seat and looked out of the window again. It was obvious that she'd forgotten about his question in all the commotion and he couldn't think of a way to raise the subject again without arousing her suspicious. Joanna would probably leap out of the cab and run off screaming into the night if she had any inkling about what he'd been thinking!

It was a deeply depressing thought so it was almost a relief when he heard the familiar sound of his beeper tweeting. He dug it out of his pocket then looked round when Joanna's beeper began to chirrup as well. 'Sounds ominous if we're both being paged,' he observed, checking the number on the display and unsurprised to find that it was the hospital paging him.

'It does.' Joanna turned off her beeper and took her mobile phone out of her bag. 'I'll find out what's going on.'

She quickly put through a call to the hospital and listened intently for a moment. 'I understand. I should be there in roughly five minutes time. Dr Archer is with me so tell the switchboard, will you? And make sure that all three Theatres are ready prepared.'

'What's happened?' Dylan asked as she ended the call and put her phone away.

'There's been a gas explosion at a block of flats near Vauxhall station.' She leant forward and told the cabby to take them to St Leonard's before continuing. 'Some of the debris landed on the station's platform so it could be some time before the exact number of casualties is known. The emergency services are talking in double figures, though.'

'Sounds grim.'

'It does. Every hospital in London has been put on standby,' she explained as the cab drew up in the hospital's forecourt. 'We're taking any patients who need immediate surgery so we'll be dealing with a real hotchpotch from the sound of it.'

'Does that include burns patients? I imagine there will be some if it's a gas explosion.' Dylan quickly paid the fare as they got out of the cab, brushing aside Joanna's offer to take care of it. Even though he was concerned about the people they would soon be treating, he found it strangely touching when she thanked him. He had a feeling that it had been some time since she'd allowed a man to take care of incidentals like cab fares which other women took for granted in a relationship.

His heart suddenly hiccuped because he was getting ahead of the game again. This wasn't a relationship. Not yet.

'They'll go to St Saviour's. We don't have the facilities here to deal with major burns cases, but they have a specialist unit there which includes an excellent plastic surgery department.'

'We'll probably have enough to keep us busy without them,' he concluded, struggling to keep his mind on work. He opened the door for Joanna then took a deep breath before he followed her into the building. Now they were here he couldn't afford to let himself be sidetracked again. The patients came first and he would make sure they had his full attention from now on.

Joanna didn't say anything else as they made their way up to Theatre. The whole floor was ablaze with lights when they stepped out of the lift and he could see staff milling about. He was aware of the interested glances he and Joanna attracted as they hurried along the corridor. The staff must know by now that he and Joanna had been together when they'd been paged and were bound to be speculating about what had been going on, but there was nothing he could do about it. Anyway, it wasn't a crime to be out with his boss.

Joanna swiftly set about organising everyone into teams. Dylan nodded when she told him he would be heading up the same team he'd worked with during that day. Tom had already changed into scrubs but he followed Dylan into the changing room, grinning broadly as he leant his massive frame against the door and watched Dylan getting ready.

'What? Or do you normally stand around at this hour of the night, grinning like the Cheshire cat?' Dylan demanded, stripping his evening shirt over his head without going through all the hassle of trying to unfasten the studs down its front.

'I'm just standing here in awe of you, oh, Great One,' Tom replied, his smile widening even more.

Dylan rolled his eyes as he unzipped his trousers and stepped out of them. 'Whilst I appreciate the fact that you obviously recognise your betters, I'm not sure what I've done to earn that accolade.'

'Oh, come now, don't be modest. I know it's supposed to be a wonderful quality but personally I've never believed you should hide your light under a bushel.'

'If I had any idea what a bushel was then maybe I'd agree with you,' he retorted, dragging on the green cotton trousers that comprised the bottom half of his Theatre garb. He picked up a top then tossed it aside when he spotted a huge rip in the side seam. Theatre clothes got a real hammering and there was nothing glamorous about the boiled-thin cotton garments which more often than not were full of holes. He selected another top off the pile and dragged it over his head then flattened down his hair with the palm of his hand.

'OK, then, I'll give up trying to be tactful, seeing as you obviously don't appreciate subtlety. What's the secret of your success with our lovely boss? Believe me, man, people have tried—and failed *miserably*—to get that woman to go out with them, yet along you come and sweep her off her dainty little feet!' Tom suddenly dropped to his knees and began genuflecting. 'Impart the secret to me, oh, Great One. Let me share this wondrous talent you have that I, too, might earn my lady's love.'

'Get up, you idiot!' Dylan began, then stopped when there was a knock on the door before Joanna poked her head into the room. He saw her mouth drop open when she spotted Tom, spread-eagled on the floor at his feet, and shook his head.

'Don't ask. You really don't want to know,' he assured her, thinking how true that statement was. Joanna would be mortified if she found out what Tom had said and he thanked heaven that the other man had kept his voice down this time.

'Oh, right. Um…A and E has just been on the phone. Can you go and take a look at a patient? They need an opinion on whether or not he will survive surgery.'

'Will do.'

'Thanks. I'll be in Theatre two if you need me.' She shot another look at Tom, who was still sprawled on the floor, opened her mouth to say something then obviously thought better of it and left.

Dylan grinned unsympathetically as Tom scrambled to his feet looking thoroughly embarrassed. 'It's your own fault.'

'I know, I know, so don't go rubbing it in,' Tom grumbled as he made for the door. 'Anyway, I'll go and do what I'm good at and leave you to carry on with your charm offensive. It's obviously working because Joanna would *never* have let me get away with that before you arrived on the scene.'

'Some people don't know when to stop,' Dylan retorted, double-knotting the cord on his pants as he followed Tom into the corridor.

'So long as you don't stop the good work then I'll put up with the insults,' Tom said loftily, waving a laconic hand as he disappeared into Theatre three.

Dylan sighed as he made his way to the lift. The situation was getting out of hand. He wasn't offended by Tom's teasing but he would hate any gossip to get back to Joanna. She would be terribly embarrassed if she realised her staff were making such personal remarks about her. Not that there was a grain of truth in what Tom had said, of course, because he couldn't in all honesty claim that he'd brought about any changes in her attitude in such a short space of time.

He got into the lift and punched the button for the ground floor, vowing that from that point on his mind would be solely on work. Not only did he owe it to the patients to give them one hundred per cent commitment but he certainly didn't want to let Joanna down when she had such high expectations of her team.

He sighed because being a worthy member of the

team wasn't the only thing he wanted to be in her eyes. He wanted her to think of him as much more than that, but at the present moment he would have to put such ideas on the back burner. He got out of the lift and headed for the accident and emergency unit, thinking wryly that the problem with that was they would just keep simmering away.

'What's his BP now?'

Joanna paused while Terry Griffith, who was her anaesthetist that night, rattled out the reading. It was very low but at least the patient still had some pressure, which was something.

She bent over the table again, wondering if she was wasting her time. Noel Price had been in bed when the gas main had exploded. He'd been almost buried by falling masonry when the ceiling had caved in on top of him and his insides were a mess. His liver, stomach, duodenum and pancreas had all been crushed. Joanna knew that his chances of recovering from such horrendous injuries were very slim but she carried on anyway, carefully removing a damaged section of his stomach. The old adage about where there was life there was hope might be trite but it was also true.

Three hours later, she finished packing the wound and straightened her aching back. She had decided to leave the wound open because there was a strong risk of infection setting in owing to the stomach's contents spilling into the abdominal cavity. If the patient survived she would stitch up the incision in a few days' time.

'That's about all we can do for now. What's his BP, Terry.'

'Would you believe it's slightly up?' Terry sounded surprised and Joanna smiled.

'It's a miracle, isn't it? Thanks, everyone. We'll take five before the next one. I think we could all do with a breather.'

A chorus of heartfelt agreements followed her out of Theatre. There was a list taped to the wall by the door, giving the names of all the patients who were still waiting for surgery, and she grimaced when she saw that there were still three people left. It was almost four a.m. and she longed to go home to her bed, but it looked as though it would be some time yet before she could leave.

She stripped off her soiled gown and tossed it into the overflowing laundry hamper then went to scrub up again. Her hands were raw from all the antiseptic she had used on them that night and she winced when the hot water stung her skin.

'One of the hazards of the job,' Lucy observed sympathetically as she joined Joanna at the sinks. 'Oh, to have lily-white hands as smooth and soft as swansdown, eh?'

'Fat chance of that in our line of work,' Joanna agreed, reaching for the nailbrush.

'What we need are a couple of handsome millionaires to take us away from this life of pain and drudgery,' Lucy declared, then glanced round when the scrub room door opened. 'Ooh, d'you think our wish is about to be granted?'

'I doubt it!' Joanna laughed as she glanced over her shoulder. She felt her breath catch when she saw that Dylan had come into the room and quickly turned back to the sink.

'So do I, unless Dr Archer here is keeping any secrets from us,' the irrepressible Lucy continued. 'Are you, Dylan?'

'That all depends on what you want to know,' he retorted as he came over to join them.

'We were just wishing that we could be swept off our feet by a couple of millionaires who would save us from this life of drudgery,' Lucy informed him airily. 'So if you happen to have the odd million or two hidden away under your bed, now is the time to confess.'

'Sorry, but I'm afraid I can't help you. I'm just a poor, hard-working medico like the rest of you.'

'Just our luck, eh, Joanna? Next time you hire someone don't forget to do a proper check on his background. There must be *some* surgeons out there whose family are millionaires!'

Lucy chuckled as she went away to fetch some more towels. Joanna shut off the taps, wondering what Dylan must think about her indulging in such a ridiculous conversation.

'So you fancy meeting a millionaire, do you?'

'It was just a bit of fun,' she replied shortly, going to the shelf for a towel before remembering they had run out. She shook her hands to air-dry them then looked up when Dylan laughed.

'I'm just trying to picture you giving all this up so you can sit by a swimming pool all day and sip Margaritas. It doesn't seem to be quite your scene, I have to say.'

'It isn't. I enjoy my job far too much to give it up.'

'I can tell.'

There was a husky note in his voice that made the hair on her arms stand to attention and she shivered. She wasn't sure how the atmosphere had become so *intimate* all of a sudden. The last place on earth anyone would describe as an intimate setting was a hospital scrub room, for heaven's sake, yet she could feel the tension swirling around her, making her feel so aware of the man who was standing a few feet away from her that her heart began to pound. It was difficult to respond when she realised that Dylan had said something to her.

'I'm sorry, what was that?'

'I just asked if you could tape up this top for me?' He twisted round so that Joanna could see the huge rip in the back of the garment. 'It was the last one left on the shelf so it's this or nothing, basically.'

'Of course. I'll just find some tape…'

'I've got some. Here you go.'

He handed her a roll of tape then turned round. Joanna tore off a strip then pulled the edges of the cotton together ready to tape them in place. Her fingers brushed the warm skin on his bare back and it felt as though she had been struck by lightning when she felt a sizzling sensation shoot from her head right the way down to her toes.

Her hands stilled, her fingers lightly splayed across Dylan's back. She was an expert on the feel of skin and tissue but she'd never felt anything as smooth and sensual as this. One fingertip began exploring, tracing a path up his spine, following the ridges of bone that felt so hard beneath the satin softness, and her breath caught. Dylan's body was made of flesh, blood and bone just like any other person's yet the description couldn't begin to explain how it felt when she touched him. It defied all description just as it defied all logic.

He slowly turned and Joanna's hands fell to her sides when she saw the expression in his eyes, all that awareness and tenderness. Dylan understood how she felt because he felt it, too, but was that justification enough to do something about what seemed to be happening? Could physical need—and there was no doubt in her mind that what she was feeling was desire—be enough to make her forget how dangerous it would be to get involved with him?

What it all came down to was one simple question: was she prepared to compromise her career and everything she had achieved for a few hours of pleasure?

CHAPTER FIVE

DYLAN could feel his heart pounding. He glanced down, half expecting to see some physical evidence of what was happening inside him, but there was no visible sign of the emotional turmoil he was experiencing.

His eyes returned to Joanna's face and his legs seemed to turn to water when he saw the expression it held. He had always considered himself to be a fairly good judge of people and that, more often than not, he could tell what they were thinking. Nevertheless, he had no idea what was going through Joanna's head at that moment and the realisation scared him half to death. He needed to stop her doing anything rash, like cutting short their burgeoning feelings for one another before she'd given him the chance to prove how good it could be between them.

'Joanna, you must listen,' he began desperately, then broke off with a muffled groan of frustration when the door bounced back against the wall as Lucy elbowed her way into the room.

'Would you believe these are the last sterile towels left in the entire hospital?' the sister announced in disgust, dumping the linen onto a shelf. 'It turns out that the firm who's supposed to provide them didn't deliver yesterday so we've run out!'

Dylan saw Joanna blink as though she'd been woken from a trance. He ached to say something but there was nothing he could do with the other woman standing there. He could hardly declare his feelings when it would only embarrass Joanna.

He gritted his teeth, wondering when he would be able to recapture the mood. Joanna had been caught off guard but it wouldn't happen again, he realised as he watched her both physically and mentally drawing back. Maybe she had been affected by his nearness and the fact that she'd been touching him—he had to pause at this point and take a deep breath when he remembered her fingertip travelling along his spine— but he knew it wouldn't happen again because she would be wary in future. It was so frustrating that he could have beaten his head against the wall only that certainly wouldn't have done anything to inspire her confidence. He had to convince her to trust him with her heart as much as she trusted him with her patients. The thought was so mind-blowingly deep that he might have keeled over if Lucy hadn't unwittingly come to his aid.

'Just look at the state of that scrub suit. It's an absolute disgrace! Here, I'll tape it together for you but something needs to be done about those suppliers.' She took the roll of tape from Joanna and briskly taped his top together. 'There. That should at least preserve your modesty, Dr Archer.'

'Thanks.' He managed to dredge up a smile but it was a poor effort. He looked round when Joanna suddenly marched to the door, realising that he had to say something before she left. He didn't want her getting upset about what had happened just now. 'Joanna…'

'I'm going to phone Adrian Watts and get him to do something about this.' She quite deliberately cut him off, making it clear that she didn't want to hear what he had to say. Dylan's nostrils flared as he fought to control his impatience. He would just have to try and sort things out at a later date although he knew it was going to be an uphill struggle.

Joanna ignored him as she turned to Lucy. 'Will you let everyone know what's happening? I shouldn't be more than ten minutes but I'm not prepared to put up with this situation any longer. It's bad enough when staff have to wear torn clothing but when patients' lives are being put at risk because of inadequate supplies then it's unforgivable.'

'Of course.' Lucy grimaced as Joanna left the room. 'Oh, dear, it sounds as though Adrian is going to get an earful. Mind you, he deserves it. The whole supply system has gone to the dogs since he took over.' She glanced at the clock and chuckled. 'Ten minutes past four. I bet he gets another ear-bashing from his wife about them being woken up at this unearthly hour!'

Dylan murmured something but he was glad when Lucy hurried off to tell the others what was happening. He scrubbed up then went back into Theatre and worked steadily until six o'clock. He dispatched the final patient to the recovery bay then went to get dressed. It didn't seem worth going home when he was on duty at eight but he needed a breathing space, time to get the smell of antiseptic out of his nostrils and thoughts of Joanna out of his mind. He would be a basket case unless he managed to put this situation into perspective.

The January morning was bitterly cold and dark when he left the hospital a short time later. The streetlamps were still lit but there were few people about. He strolled along the road until he came to the park and on a sudden whim went in and sat on a bench near the gate. It was really too cold to sit outside at this time of the year but the icy air felt good after the artificial warmth in Theatre.

He breathed in deeply, filling his lungs with air that was fresher than what he'd left behind even if it didn't have that quality much beloved by poets of tasting of wine. Essence of diesel was a better description of London's air!

A smile curled his mouth at the thought and he was still smiling when a woman suddenly appeared. Dylan watched her hesitate outside the gate then slowly come into the park, and in a funny way realised that he'd been half expecting this to happen. That Joanna should have had the same idea as him after the hectic night they'd had seemed only fitting.

He stood up as she approached, wondering what she would do when she saw him. He hoped she wouldn't turn tail and leave but he would understand if she did. She was as wary of him as he was eager to get to know her and whilst that meant there was a certain balance to their relationship, it didn't bode well for harmony. All he could do was hope that she would realise he wouldn't do anything to hurt her. He would lay down his life rather than cause her any pain and it was a sobering thought, almost as sobering as the one that followed it.

He had fallen in love with Joanna Martin in the space of a single day and a night.

Joanna couldn't remember when she'd last felt so tired. She was used to the long hours that were a surgeon's lot but the weariness she felt now stemmed from an emotional as well as a physical source. What had happened in the scrub room with Dylan had shocked her to the core. She had always considered herself to be a woman who was in control of her life but for those few minutes nothing had mattered apart from the feel of his body under her hands. She'd wanted him so much that it had left a lingering ache inside her that wouldn't seem to budge, which was why she had decided to try and walk it off. Cold air and exercise were supposed to be the antidote to unrequited passion and she was putting the theory to the test.

A figure suddenly appeared in front of her and she stopped dead. All of a sudden she became uncomfortably aware that it really wasn't sensible to be wandering around a London park in the dark. She half turned to hurry back up the path when the man spoke, and the sound of his voice stole all the strength from her limbs.

'Don't go, Joanna. Please.'

It was the 'please' that did it, she thought afterwards, that note of entreaty in Dylan's voice which was impossible to resist. She glanced back and knew she was lost the moment she felt her heart race when he smiled at her. Her head might know it was dangerous to let this continue but her stubborn heart refused to listen. It was playing on the fact that she was too tired and too emotional to fight back. She stood in silence as Dylan came towards her. He stopped in front of her and it seemed the most natural thing in the world when he bent and kissed her softly on the cheek.

'Thank you for not running away,' he murmured, his voice sounding very deep and husky in the quiet of the morning. 'I wouldn't have blamed you if you had, but I do appreciate it.'

He took hold of her hand, frowning when he felt

how cold it was. 'You're freezing! Here, let me warm you up.' He laced his fingers between hers and slid both their hands into the pocket of his overcoat as he began walking along the path. Joanna shivered when she felt the warmth seeping into her. She knew she should pull her hand away but it felt too good to deprive herself of such a simple pleasure.

Her hand nestled deeper into his coat pocket and she heard Dylan let out a small sigh of contentment. For some reason it pleased her that *he* was pleased even though she couldn't understand why it should matter. It just *did* and she had to be content with that because she was far too tired to look for an explanation.

They did a full circuit of the park then stopped when they arrived back at their starting point. Dylan turned to face her and his expression was filled with tenderness when he looked into her eyes.

'It feels good to be out in the open air after the night we had, doesn't it?'

'It does.'

'Do you fancy another turn around the park or can I tempt you to a cup of coffee? There's an all-night café not far from here so we could even have some breakfast if you fancy it.'

'That sounds good,' she agreed, realising in surprise that she was hungry.

'Great!' His face broke into a grin as he spun her round and headed for the gate at top speed.

'Why the rush?' Joanna demanded, trotting along beside him in her high-heeled evening shoes, not the best kind of footwear to choose to negotiate the cracked tarmac.

'Because I'm absolutely ravenous, and if I don't get

something to eat soon I might just pass out!' he declared, not slowing down as he hustled her out of the park.

She chuckled at the fervent note in his voice. 'And after you had that wonderful dinner last night, too.'

'That was *hours* ago. Anyway, I'm not sure I agree with you about it being "a wonderful dinner".'

'Wasn't it to your liking?' she asked in surprise, because she'd really enjoyed the meal. The smoked salmon starter had been absolutely delicious, almost as good as the tender slices of duck breast nestling on an endive salad which had followed it. It had been a vast improvement on the usual hospital fare and she was rather surprised that Dylan hadn't enjoyed it.

'Oh, it was fine. There just wasn't enough of it. Nouvelle cuisine is all well and good but I prefer it when there's less of the "nouvelle" and more of the "cuisine". Having your food cut into fancy shapes might look pretty but it doesn't exactly fill you up.'

'I suppose not.' Joanna laughed again then realised that she had laughed more in the past twenty-four hours than she'd done in ages. She hurriedly chased away the thought that it was all Dylan's doing because she couldn't cope with any more evidence of the effect he had on her. 'Do I take it that this café we're going to doesn't go in for nouvelle cuisine, then?'

'You take it right.' He stopped at the kerb then hurried her across the road after he'd checked there was no traffic coming. 'They believe in serving generous portions there so I hope you're up to it?'

'If that's a challenge, Dr Archer, I accept. Anything you can eat, I can eat, too!'

'You might live to regret that,' he warned, but she shook her head.

'No chance! I could eat a horse at this precise moment.'

'Then I'll see what I can do!'

He took her arm, drawing her against him as they hurried along the street. Joanna could feel their hips bumping together as they walked and a strange feeling of security settled over her. Maybe it was silly to let herself get too close to this man but just for once she didn't want to worry about doing the right thing. Anyhow, what harm could there be in enjoying his company for a short while so long as she made it clear to him later that it had been a one-off experience?

Her heart ached when Dylan stopped outside the café and opened the door. She knew it wouldn't be easy to tell him that, but she didn't have a choice. Getting involved with Dylan would be a mistake for any number of reasons and not just because of the damage it could do to her career. It would affect the whole of her life and she wasn't ready for that, couldn't cope with the thought of having to make such massive changes. After they'd had breakfast she would make it clear that their dealings with each other had to be on a strictly professional footing in the future. It would be the best thing to do for both their sakes even though it was very hard to accept that.

'Sausage, bacon, tomatoes, fried bread, eggs… How do you like your eggs, Joanna?'

Dylan lowered the menu, hiding his smile when he saw Joanna's expression. He had offered to order for them both and was making the most of the opportunity. Was she having second thoughts about accepting his challenge? he wondered tenderly, watching her bite her lip. Or was there something else worrying her?

Alarm bells suddenly started to ring inside his head but he managed not to show how tense he felt when she looked up.

'Fried, sunny side up, please.'

'Fine. Make that a double order for both of us, please, Mario. Oh, and can you bring us some toast as well? We may as well go the whole hog.'

'*Sì, Dottore Archer.*'

The waiter hurried away, shouting their order to the cook in rapid-fire Italian. Dylan took a small breath to try and calm his nerves. Was Joanna having second thoughts about being here with him? Was she having second *and* third thoughts about the way they'd walked around the park together, her hand snugly tucked into his pocket?

He sensed it was true and sighed because it wasn't going to be easy to convince her there was nothing to worry about. She'd only known him a day and she was bound to have doubts about what seemed to be happening, but he had to find a way to reassure her. He needed her in his life and he wasn't prepared to give up at the first hurdle.

'Do you come here very often?'

A smile curled his mouth when she trotted out that old chestnut in such a serious tone. She was completely unaware of what she'd said so he answered just as seriously, not wanting to embarrass her with some kind of teasing remark. His heart jolted because he would have had no hesitation about making a joke if anyone other than Joanna had come out with that question and it just seemed to prove how special she was.

'Quite often, as you probably guessed from the fact that Mario knows my name.'

He cleared his throat when he heard the emotion in

his voice. Falling in love was something he had often wondered about in a detached kind of a way. He'd dismissed all the descriptions he'd read about bells ringing and hearts racing as a lot of foolish nonsense. Maybe people *did* experience a certain physical reaction when they met the person they wanted to spend their life with, but he'd firmly believed that it was the result of simple sexual desire. However, it wasn't just the fact that he wanted to make love to Joanna—and he did!—but he also wanted to cherish her, protect her, hear her laugh when she was happy and comfort her when she was sad. It was the whole kit and caboodle he felt, an emotional outpouring so intense that it stunned him. It was a wonder he was still able to function, in fact.

'I tend to come here whenever I've had a really heavy day and can't be bothered cooking for myself.' He cleared his throat again, worried that he would reinforce those second thoughts she was having if he didn't get a grip. 'The food is good and there's none of that nonsense you get at so many restaurants with the waiter hovering around you all the time. Mario takes your order, brings your food and leaves you in peace.'

'A real bonus,' she agreed, unbuttoning her coat and letting it fall over the back of her chair.

Dylan picked up a fork and began gouging tracks into a paper napkin while he willed himself to calm down. Joanna was wearing the same dress she'd worn for dinner the previous night and he couldn't help thinking once again how lovely she looked. The black velvet was the perfect foil for her delicate colouring, highlighting the fairness of her skin and the soft gold of her hair. A few wisps had escaped from their elegant knot and were curling around her ears, softening the rather austere image she normally projected. She was a beautiful and desirable woman and everything that was male in him responded to her in a way that was quite frankly alarming. He had always believed that people should keep their private life private, yet he could have happily swept her out of that chair, laid her down on this table and made mad, passionate love to her!

Fortunately, Mario arrived with their order just then so Dylan was spared any more torture. Silence fell as he and Joanna tucked into the food. He grinned when he saw her break off a corner of toast and dip it into her egg yolk.

'I'm glad you did that. It means I don't have to mind my manners.' Breaking off a hunk of toast, he dunked it into the runny yolk then popped it in his mouth. 'Delicious,' he mumbled appreciatively.

'I only did it because I could tell you were dying to dunk,' she declared, daintily wiping a crumb off her mouth with a napkin.

'Oh, yeah!' he scoffed. 'A likely story! You're a dyed-in-the-wool dunker. There's no point trying to deny it because I can tell!'

'Rubbish! All right, so I admit that I have been known to dunk the odd biscuit into my coffee but I have never, *ever* dunked into an egg yolk before.'

'Oh, *puhlease*!' He laid down his knife and fork and stared at her. 'Do you really expect me to believe that you haven't dipped a soldier into a boiled egg? I mean, that's like asking me to believe the world is square!'

'All right, then.' A wash of colour flowed up her face at being caught out. 'Maybe I have dipped into a *boiled* egg but I've never done the same to a fried egg, Mr Pedantic!'

'I just like to get the facts straight,' he declared, picking up his cutlery. 'It saves a lot of problems, I always find.'

'It does.'

There was a solemn note in her voice all of a sudden and Dylan felt his stomach muscles tighten when he looked up. It was obvious that she wanted to say something and he desperately didn't want to hear it until he'd got in first.

'Joanna, I need to tell you something—something important,' he began.

'Please, don't.' She smiled but there were tears in her eyes. 'I don't want to hear it, Dylan. I know that you and I have a…a certain rapport but it's not enough.'

'Not enough? What do you mean by that?' he demanded, his anger rising on the back of a sudden tide of fear.

'That it isn't enough to make me throw away everything I've worked so hard to achieve,' she said bluntly. 'If I got involved with you it would be professional suicide. I would become the butt of a lot of unsavoury gossip and I'm just not prepared to let that happen.'

'But that's crazy! Why should people gossip about us? And even if they did why should it have a detrimental effect?' He reached over the table and gripped her hand, willing her to listen to him.

'Because I'm a woman making her way in a man's world. The rules that apply to men don't apply to me. I've had to work twice as hard and twice as long to get this far, and it could all end tomorrow if I lost my credibility.' She gently withdrew her hand and he could tell that she was withdrawing from him emotionally as well. 'I am forty-two years old, Dylan, and you're what—thirty-three, thirty-four?'

'Thirty-five.'

He wanted to add something, *anything* that would convince her their ages weren't an issue, only he knew there was a grain of truth in what she'd said. Nobody thought twice about a man having a relationship with a younger female colleague—it was an accepted fact of life. However, the age gap between him and Joanna could arouse a lot of speculation, especially when he worked for her. He'd seen it happen before, seen the heartache it had caused for the couple concerned. They had split up because they hadn't been able to deal with the narrow-minded attitude of their colleagues, but surely he and Joanna could rise above it? If only she would give him a chance to prove to her that what they had outweighed everything else…

But did it? Could it *really* compensate for the fact that her career might be damaged? He might feel strongly about Joanna but there was no proof that she felt anything for him.

Defeat was something that Dylan had never experienced before and it left a bitter taste in his mouth now. When Joanna pushed back her chair, he didn't attempt to stop her because he could tell that it would be a waste of time. Maybe if they'd had the chance to get to know one another he would have been able to persuade her to let him try and find a solution to the problem, but this whole situation had sprung up out of nowhere. How could he expect her to trust him to look after her interests when she'd known him barely a day?

'It's time I went home to change. Thank you for breakfast, I enjoyed it.' She slipped on her coat and he saw her fingers fumble as she fastened the buttons and knew she wasn't as composed as she was trying to pretend.

He stood up and walked around the table, taking her trembling hands in his as he pulled her into his arms and held her—just held her—before he let her go. And there was a lump in his throat and an ache in his heart he couldn't even attempt to hide when he said softly, 'Take care going home, won't you?'

'I shall.' There was a second when he thought she was going to say something else before she reached up and kissed him on the cheek. 'I'll see you later, Dr Archer.'

Dylan didn't try to detain her as she left the café. There was no point. He sat down again but the food tasted like sawdust now. He asked Mario for the bill and left the café a few minutes later, checking his watch as he made his way to the tube. It was just gone seven, twenty-three hours since he'd started his new job. It wasn't very long, certainly not long enough by most people's standards to have fallen in love *and* had his heart broken. Now he had to accept that Joanna was never going to be his and get on with his life.

He grimaced because it wasn't going to be easy when he would have to see her every day at work. He would just have to do his best—for both their sakes.

CHAPTER SIX

'I WISH I could promise you that your husband will make a full recovery, Mrs Price, but the injuries he received were very serious indeed.'

Joanna had been on her way to her office after the morning ward round had finished when the IC unit had paged to tell her that Noel Price's wife was asking to speak to her. The IC consultant was on holiday that week so Joanna had agreed to have a word with the woman in his absence.

Kathleen Price had been staying overnight with her mother when the explosion had ripped through the block of flats and had only discovered that her husband had been injured when she'd returned home that morning. She was dreadfully upset and Joanna sighed as she took her into the relatives' room because it was obvious that she was going to have to spend far more time than she could spare, talking to her.

'I just can't believe what's happened!' Kathleen Price exclaimed, sinking down onto a chair. 'I mean, everything was fine when I left home last night. Mum's had a dreadful cold, you see, and Noel knew I was worried about her so he told me to stay the night with her. I couldn't believe my eyes when I saw the state of the place this morning. It looked like a bomb site!'

'It must have been a terrible shock,' Joanna sympathised, shooting a surreptitious glance at her watch. Last night's emergency had put a lot of pressure on everyone and they were still suffering the after-effects. The ward round had taken twice as long as it normally did because there'd been so many extra patients to see, plus there were several people who would need to be taken back to Theatre later that day. They would have to be fitted in around the operations that were already scheduled but it looked as though it was going to be another hectic session.

'Oh, it was!' Kathleen agreed. 'But the worst thing of all was seeing Noel lying in that bed. He looks so ill!'

She began to sob as Joanna sat down beside her. 'I know how frightening it must have been to see your husband attached to all that machinery, Mrs Price, but this really is the best place for him.'

'I know that, Doctor. Really, I do. It was just such a shock, you understand.' Kathleen wiped her eyes. 'I'm sorry. I'm not helping matters by falling apart like this. Tell me, honestly, what are Noel's chances of pulling through?'

Joanna hesitated but she knew it would be wrong to raise Mrs Price's hopes. It was best to tell people the truth rather than mislead them into thinking everything was going to be fine.

Her heart spasmed with pain because that thought reminded her about what had happened earlier that morning between her and Dylan. She *could* have suggested that they should be circumspect and make sure that no one found out they were seeing each other, but she knew it would have been the wrong thing to do. There was just no way that she could risk getting involved with Dylan. It wouldn't be fair to him or to herself. She was his boss and he was a member of her team—that had to be the sum total of their relationship from now on even though it wouldn't be easy to stick that. There was something about Dylan that drew her as no other man had ever done.

Joanna put that worrying thought out of her mind as she gently explained to Kathleen Price how gravely ill her husband was. 'Your husband's injuries were very severe, Mrs Price. I had to remove sections of his stomach and pancreas when I operated on him.'

'But will he pull through?' Kathleen persisted. 'He can live with bits of his insides missing?'

'Yes, he can.' Joanna held up her hand when Kathleen gasped in relief. 'However, even if he does pull through, and it is *if* at this stage, there could be problems in the future. I had to remove the head of the pancreas so there is a strong possibility that he might develop diabetes because the pancreas won't be able to produce enough insulin. Obviously, there is a high risk of infection with this type of injury, too, although he is currently receiving antibiotics to counteract that.' She shrugged. 'Add shock and extensive blood loss and you can see that he is a very sick man.'

'I understand that, Doctor, but he has a chance and that's all that matters.' Kathleen took a deep breath and stood up. 'You've done all you can for him and I'm truly grateful to you. Now it's my turn. I'm going back in there and I'm going to make him fight to get better!'

'Good for you.' Joanna smiled when she heard the determination in the woman's voice. 'I'm a firm believer in the power of positive thought so, who knows, you might just give your husband that extra little incentive he needs.'

'That's what I intend to do.'

Kathleen hurried on ahead as they left the room and

went straight into the IC unit. Joanna paused to have a brief word with the sister then went to her office. She checked her messages then headed to Theatre when she discovered there was nothing needing her urgent attention. Sarah Rothwell, one of her junior registrars, was talking to Dylan outside Theatre one. Joanna nodded to them as she passed, trying to ignore the pang of jealousy that had struck her when she'd seen Dylan chatting to the younger woman. Dylan was free to talk to whomsoever he chose and it had nothing to do with her.

That thought was all well and good but it was hard to remain upbeat when she left Theatre a couple of hours later and found Dylan and Sarah deep in conversation once more. She shot them a withering look as she strode towards the changing room.

'If you two are short of work I'm sure I can find something to occupy you,' she said coldly.

'Dylan was just explaining what to look out for when I do this appendicectomy that's been rushed in,' Sarah said hurriedly.

'If you have problems about performing a simple appendicectomy, Dr Rothwell, I suggest you discuss them with me. We may need to review your position as a member of this team.'

The door slammed shut behind her as Joanna let herself into the changing room. She knew she'd been rather hard on the younger woman but there was no room on the team for people who suffered from a lack of confidence. If Sarah had to double-check before such a simple procedure maybe she was in the wrong job.

She had tossed her disposable cap into the trash bag

and was just about to kick off her Theatre shoes when the door opened and Dylan appeared.

'There was no need to take it out on Sarah.'

'I've no idea what you're talking about. Now, if you don't mind, Dr Archer, I am trying to get changed.'

He ignored her as he closed the door and leant against it with his arms folded. There was a glint in his eyes that warned her he was angry about what had happened, but she was angry, too. A couple of hours ago he'd been turning on the charm for *her* benefit and it hurt to realise just how quickly he'd set his sights on someone else after she'd rebuffed him. Obviously, Dylan wasn't suffering from a broken heart!

'If it's me you're angry with then why not say so, Joanna? It isn't fair to bite Sarah's head off because I've rubbed you up the wrong way.'

'I didn't bite Sarah's head off nor did you *rub me up the wrong way*! How I deal with my staff is my business and I don't think you are in any position to comment.'

'Oh, come on. We both know what this is all about!' He laughed harshly. 'You're annoyed with me because I dared to overstep the mark this morning. You're also angry at yourself because you let your guard slip, and that's even more unforgivable, isn't it? I'm willing to accept my share of the blame so why can't you accept yours?'

'You have it all worked out, don't you, Dr Archer? How wonderful it must be to have such a rare insight into what makes a person tick.' Her laughter was filled with scorn and she saw his mouth thin.

'I don't have anything worked out. I'm simply adding two and two and hoping to find an answer that makes some sense. I can't see any other reason why you would choose to destroy Sarah's confidence like that. I don't think you're a naturally cruel person but, then, I don't know you that well, do I?'

'No, you don't.'

Joanna turned away when she felt the hot sting of tears fill her eyes. Had she dented Sarah's confidence by her comments? She hated to think it was true but there was no way that she could simply dismiss the claim. Didn't she know how hard it was for a woman to make her way in surgery, how difficult it was to fight against the sexist culture that still thrived in so many hospitals? The thought that she might be guilty of inflicting that kind of harm on the younger woman was hard to accept but she had to face what she had done and try to make amends.

'I shall apologise to Dr Rothwell as soon as I get the chance,' she said, her voice muffled with tears of shame. 'I didn't mean to upset her.'

'And I didn't mean to upset you, either.'

Suddenly Dylan was behind her, his hands warm and strong on her shoulders as he turned her to face him. He sighed when he saw the tears trembling on her lashes. 'I'm sorry, Joanna. I overreacted just now. Will you forgive me?'

'There's nothing to forgive,' she said huskily. 'It was my fault for snapping like that. It was just when I saw you and Sarah…'

She stopped and swallowed but he had already guessed what she'd been about to say. A wave of sadness crossed his face as he drew her to him and hugged her tightly for a moment before he let her go.

'I'm sorry. It almost makes me wish that I'd never started this,' he said simply.

Joanna didn't say anything as he left the changing room. Pointing out that he'd said he was *almost* sorry wouldn't have helped the situation one bit. However, the thought that Dylan didn't regret what had happened stayed with her for the rest of the day, a small bright spot that shone out through the gloom. Maybe they couldn't be anything more than colleagues but the fact that he didn't regret how he felt took away some of the ache. In a funny kind of a way she knew how he felt because she wasn't sorry about what had happened either. How strange.

Dylan was surprised by how easily he and Joanna managed to overcome their initial difficulties during the ensuing weeks. He knew she was making as much of an effort as he was to keep everything on an even keel but he'd still expected there to be hiccups. Maybe it was the fact that they were meticulous about keeping any conversations they had on a purely work-related footing that helped.

Several times he found himself mentally taking a step back while he was talking to Joanna and observing what was happening. He could scarcely believe that he could remain so focused on work when he felt so strongly about her. But, then, he didn't have a choice. It was either play the game according to her rules or find himself another job, and he simply wasn't prepared to cut himself off from her completely. Maybe it was foolish but he couldn't stop hoping that one day she would see that they could have a future together that wasn't solely work-orientated.

February came and went, then March arrived and he was busier than ever. St Leonard's reputation was spreading and they were getting a lot of referrals from

GPs within their catchment area. Joanna's weekly clinics—when she assessed new patients who might require surgery—were filled to overflowing and he wasn't surprised when she arranged for him to hold a second clinic to share the workload. Wednesday afternoon was the time set aside for referrals and he'd just settled down to check through his list when she popped her head round the consulting room door.

'Brian Maxwell has just been on the phone to ask me if I'd go to his office,' she explained, referring to the hospital's director. 'It means I might be a bit late starting today so could you take a couple of my patients if you're not too busy?'

'Of course, although I've got a pretty full list myself today, too.' He tapped the printed sheet that was lying on his desk. 'There's four people been referred to us by that new GP at the health centre along the road for starters.'

'He seems to be drumming up a lot of business for us lately.'

She came over to the desk so she could read the list of names and the reasons why the patients had been referred to them. Dylan felt his heart jolt when she bent and he caught the faint aroma of her soap—something delicate and feminine that made his insides quiver with delight. It was difficult to hide how it made him feel when she glanced up, and the sudden rush of colour that invaded her cheeks pointed to the fact that he hadn't been completely successful in his efforts.

'Quite a variety from the look of it, although I do wonder if the GP has tried an alternative remedy for that case of carpal tunnel syndrome,' she said quietly, obviously determined to stick to work matters.

'I wondered about that, too,' Dylan agreed, trying

his hardest not to make the situation more fraught than it was. It wasn't fair to Joanna to put her under any kind of pressure, but it was difficult to hide his feelings when she was near him. 'I felt that he might have been jumping the gun with a couple of the patients he's referred to us recently, to be honest.'

'In that case we'd better monitor the situation. It isn't unknown for a busy GP to pass patients along because he hasn't the time to work out a suitable course of treatment for them.'

'It happened in my last post, too. Mind you, the GP was also sending patients to the accident and emergency unit rather than seeing them himself.' He sighed. 'It turned out that he had a drink problem and couldn't keep up with his workload.'

'There's tremendous pressure on GPs nowadays, especially in a city like London where the population is increasing all the time. However, much as I sympathise, there is no way that we can pick up another doctor's work.'

'I'll keep a check on how many new patients are coming from the health centre,' he assured her.

'Thanks.' She gave him a quick smile then went to the door. She paused and glanced back. 'I'll be as quick as I can but page me if you get snowed under. Brian tends to be extremely long-winded once he gets started.'

'I'll give you half an hour then send for the cavalry,' he assured her, grinning.

Joanna chuckled. 'You may need to, believe me!'

She left and Dylan got back to what he'd been doing. He liked to have some idea of the cases he would be seeing before the patients arrived so tried to spend some time beforehand going through their notes. He was just reading up on the carpal tunnel syndrome case when his beeper sounded and he grimaced when he discovered it was A and E paging him.

He phoned the department to find out what was happening and agreed immediately to look at a ten-year-old boy who had been run over by a bus. He quickly left the consulting room and stopped at the reception desk to tell the staff where he was going. There was already a queue of patients waiting to be seen but they would have to wait a while longer because this call took priority.

The child was very badly injured and Dylan didn't hesitate as he phoned Theatre to inform the staff that he would be operating. He then phoned the clinic to alert them to the fact that he wouldn't be able to see any of his appointments for at least two hours. It would probably mean them rebooking appointments if Joanna wasn't able to cover for him, but it couldn't be helped.

Dylan apologised for the inconvenience and hung up. He hurried to the lift, working out which way to approach the coming surgery. A and E had provided him with a full set of X-rays so he knew the boy's pelvis was broken in three places and suspected from the traces of blood in the child's urine that his bladder had been damaged. It would be a test of his skill to put everything back together but he was confident that he would make a success of it. As Tom was so fond of saying, false modesty was a waste of time and he was well aware of his own strengths. He wouldn't do this job if there was the slightest doubt in his mind that he wasn't any good at it.

The lift arrived almost as soon as he pressed the button for once. He was just about to get in when he spotted Joanna coming along the corridor and he put out his hand to stop the lift door closing.

'I've an emergency,' he informed her quickly. 'Ten-year-old boy who had an argument with a bus. Pelvis is broken in three places and I suspect his bladder has been damaged as well. I'm not sure how long I'll be, probably a couple of hours minimum.'

'Oh…um… Fine. Don't worry. I'll cover for you.'

Dylan frowned when he saw how abstracted she looked. It was obvious that she had something on her mind. 'What's wrong? Did Brian Maxwell give you some bad news about the department?'

'No. Just the opposite, in fact.' She summoned a smile but he couldn't help noticing how she avoided looking directly at him. 'I'll tell you all about it later. You'd better get off to Theatre and I'd better make a start before the natives get restless.'

He laughed at the quip but he couldn't help feeling a little unsettled because something obviously wasn't right. 'Heaven forbid! I'll see you later, then.'

He let go of the door and the last thing he saw before it closed was the frown on Joanna's face. He was dying to know what was bothering her but it would have to wait. Still, it couldn't be anything that dreadful because she would have told him there and then. It was probably some sort of management crisis, maybe to do with the figures everyone was so keen on nowadays.

He sighed. When folk started measuring the effectiveness of a department by the number of operations performed there then the whole system had well and truly broken down! No wonder Joanna had looked so dismayed.

*   *   *

'I'm going to write to your GP, Miss Rogers, and suggest that he injects a small dose of corticosteroid drugs under the ligament in your right wrist. That should relieve the pain, but do follow my advice and use a splint at night to rest your hand.'

It had been a hectic couple of hours and Joanna hadn't stopped as she had worked her way through the list of patients who'd been booked in that day. Adding Dylan's list to her own had taken some juggling but she had managed to keep up, mainly because she had worked like a Trojan rather than given herself time to think about the bombshell Brian Maxwell had dropped.

A shiver ran through her and she had to consciously blank the thought from her head because she couldn't deal with it at that moment. Debbie Rogers, the patient suffering from carpal tunnel syndrome, was obviously relieved to learn there was an alternative to surgery and said so.

'I'll try anything if it means that I don't need to have an operation! I was terrified when Dr Brooks told me he was referring me to the hospital. I only went to ask him for some painkillers, and before I knew what was happening, he was talking about me having surgery!'

'I see.' Joanna managed to hide her dismay because it seemed that Dylan's suspicions were correct. The new doctor at the health centre was referring patients to them to ease his own workload.

'I really think it's a bit too soon to think about surgery, Miss Rogers. Carpal tunnel syndrome can be very painful but it can be treated by other means. The pain is the result of pressure on the median nerve where it passes into the hand through the carpal tunnel.

It's quite common in people who work for long periods of time on word processors or computers, although that isn't the only cause, by any means.'

'It's probably what's caused my problem, though,' Debbie stated glumly. 'I design websites for a living and spend hours a day working on a computer.'

'Then do make sure you have the very best, ergonomically designed equipment to help ease the pressure on your wrists. And try to take frequent breaks away from your computer.' She smiled when the young woman grimaced. 'I know it isn't easy when it's your job but if your wrist gets too painful then you won't be able to do any work at all.'

'I suppose you're right,' Debbie agreed reluctantly. She stood up. 'I'll try to be sensible about it from now on. And I'll make another appointment with my GP and ask him for that injection you mentioned.'

'I shall write to him and let him know to expect you,' Joanna assured her.

Debbie Rogers left and Joanna saw two more patients, one of whom was another referral from the health centre who should have been treated with the right combination of drugs rather than surgery. Once again she explained that she would contact the GP about a suitable course of treatment although this patient obviously wasn't as happy about the idea as Debbie had been.

She sighed as the man stamped out of the room, muttering about the state of the NHS and doctors who were more interested in feathering their nests than doing their jobs properly. There was no point explaining that he should never have been referred to her in the first place because he wouldn't have believed her, but it was frustrating. When the nurse who was assisting

her that afternoon suggested that she might like a cup
of coffee, Joanna eagerly agreed. A break would give
her time to unwind.

She was just sipping the hot coffee when there was
a tap on the door and Dylan poked his head around it.
'Coffee? I thought you'd be in dire need of a stiff
whisky by now.'

'I am, but I don't think the powers that be would
approve of me drinking alcohol on the job.'

She summoned a smile as he came into the room,
trying to calm the sudden thundering of her heart.
He'd obviously come straight from Theatre because
his hair was still wet from the shower. Joanna felt her
pulse race as she imagined how his hair would feel if
she ran her fingers through it. It would be like stroking
damp black satin, she thought, and the idea made her
insides spasm with longing.

She took a deep breath, struggling against feelings
she had no right to feel. Dylan was a colleague. He
was her senior registrar and she was his boss. Thinking
about stroking his hair was a lot of foolish nonsense,
especially after what Brian Maxwell had told her earlier.

The cup slipped from her fingers, spattering coffee
onto the immaculate blotter before she managed to
right it. Joanna reached for a tissue and quickly
mopped up the mess but her heart seemed to have
gone into her overdrive. She would have to tell Dylan
what Brian had said although she had no idea how to
set about it.

'That was clumsy of me!' she exclaimed, playing
for time. 'How did you get on, by the way? Was the
boy in a very bad state?'

'He was. It turned out that his bladder must have

ruptured when he was hit by the bus. It's pretty common with that kind of accident. I managed to sew it back together and pin his pelvis so I'm hoping there won't be any long-term problems like incontinence or urine retention, but it's too early to tell if there's been much nerve damage.' He looked at her enquiringly. 'How did you get on? I was surprised to see so few people left in the waiting room.'

'There were no real problems and that helped,' she said quickly, not wanting to admit why she had worked with such gusto.

'What about the carpal tunnel syndrome?'

'It appears the GP referred her to us without suggesting corticosteroid injections, or much else for that matter.' Joanna swiftly filled him in on what had happened both with Debbie Rogers and the other patient. She nodded when Dylan declared that something needed to be done about the situation.

'I intend to get onto it as soon as I've finished here. We're busy enough, without the GPs foisting extra patients onto us.' She looked up when the nurse knocked to ask her if she was ready to see her next patient.

'You can send the next one in as soon as you like,' she told her.

'And if you give me a couple of minutes to get myself sorted out you can start ferrying the rest to me, too,' Dylan instructed. He sighed as he made for the door as soon as the nurse had left. 'I'd better go and do my bit, I suppose. Thanks for covering for me, Joanna.'

He reached for the doorhandle then stopped. 'By the way, you said you'd tell me what Brian Maxwell wanted. I hope he wasn't complaining about the figures.'

'He wasn't. In fact, he had absolutely no complaints at all and was positively lavish with his compliments.'

Joanna hesitated but there was no way she could put this off any longer. Dylan had to know what had been said, although how he would react was anyone's guess.

'Apparently, Brian and the members of the trust are delighted with our performance. It turns out that we've performed more operations than any other surgical unit in our area in the past three months, *and* that our success rate is twenty per cent higher than anyone else's as well.'

'That's brilliant news, Joanna! Well done. It's all down to you that St Leonard's has improved so dramatically.'

'Thank you, but I see it more as a team effort. Every single person on this team is responsible for the improvement in the quality of the surgery we perform here.' She took a small breath because this was the bit she was dreading telling him. 'Brian is so delighted, in fact, that he wants us to attend the conference in Paris next month and present a paper on how we have raised the standards here so successfully. It's an all-expenses-paid trip and we've been booked into one of the best hotels right next to the conference centre.'

'We? I'm not sure I understand what you're saying, Joanna,' he said slowly.

'It's simple. Brian wants us both to go to Paris. Together.'

CHAPTER SEVEN

'I SEE. And how do you feel about the idea?'

Dylan was rather proud of the fact that his voice sounded so normal. He fixed what he hoped would appear to be a professional smile to his mouth while he waited for Joanna to answer, but it was difficult to be sure that he wasn't grinning like a kid who'd just been handed a treat. The thought of going to Paris with Joanna, for whatever reason, made his blood sing, but he had to get it into perspective.

It would be a business trip.

They would be in Paris purely and simply so they could present a paper to their learned colleagues.

If they had to socialise they would do so in the company of other professionals.

There would be no time for anything except work…

Unless they managed to sneak in a moonlit trip up the Seine and a walk around the Tuileries Gardens. And, of course, they *couldn't* go to Paris without seeing the Eiffel Tower and the Louvre, could they? It would be tantamount to committing a cardinal sin to miss either of those! OK, so maybe he *had* been before and seen all the major sights, but he had never seen them with Joanna and that made a world of difference…

'Obviously, I'm pleased that the trust appreciates all our hard work but I'm not sure I agree with the fact that they are prepared to spend so much money on this jaunt which could be put to better use elsewhere.'

96

Dylan blinked and the delightful images of Paris in the spring faded as he digested what she'd said. She had sounded so *professional* that he felt like an idiot for letting himself get carried away. It wasn't a feeling he enjoyed so he fought to suppress it by taking the opposite tack. Maybe he wasn't convinced it would be wise for them to go to Paris together but he wasn't going to let Joanna think that he was incapable of handling the experience. If she wanted professional then that's what she was going to get. In spades!

'I disagree. The cost of the trip is a mere drop in the ocean when you weigh it against the benefits St Leonard's will gain from it.' His tone was calm, composed and completely convincing, and even he was faintly surprised by what a good actor he was turning out to be. Joanna was obviously taken aback by his performance because she was silent for a moment before she rallied.

'What sort of benefits do you mean?'

'That the department's reputation can only be enhanced even further by the fact that we've been asked to deliver this paper.'

He was winging it now—snatching ideas off the top of his head so he could convince her that they should go ahead with the trip. If there were problems then he would get round them, he promised himself. He would find a way to make it work because he needed this time with Joanna more than he had needed anything in his entire life.

'There's been talk recently about more hospitals being designated as centres of excellence and St Leonard's surgical department would be a prime candidate for extra government funding. Just imagine the

massive boost that would give to the quality of care
we provide here.'

'Brian Maxwell did mention something along those
lines,' she admitted slowly. 'He said that the board of
Trustees was very keen to capitalise on our success
and apply for extra funding. He also said that it could
have a knock-on effect for the whole hospital so there
might be extra funding made available to other de-
partments.'

'Exactly.' He shrugged, feeling rather pleased that
he had read the situation so well. He had never got
too heavily involved with the politics of the job in the
past because he'd not been in a position to do so.
However, at his present level, he was more than willing to add his ten cents' worth, and once he became
a consultant he would definitely fight his corner.

His heart jolted because undoubtedly he would have
to change jobs if he hoped to become a consultant. St
Leonard's already had a consultant on its surgical
team, and a highly skilled one, too, by all accounts.
He hadn't met Diane Grant yet because she was currently on maternity leave, but he had been told that
she would be returning to work very shortly. He hated
the thought of having to leave Joanna for any reason
and hurried on, not wanting to think about the downside of moving up the professional ladder.

'Maxwell knows that the only way you can get hold
of extra funding is by building on your reputation and
that's why he's so keen that you should go to this
conference. It makes a lot of sense.'

'I suppose it does when you put it like that. And I
would love to think that one day this department
would have sufficient funding to be at the cutting edge

of surgery.' She grimaced at the unwitting pun. 'Sorry, but you know what I mean, don't you?'

'I do,' he agreed, chuckling.

'So basically we both agree it would be the right thing for us to do professionally, but how do you feel about it personally?' A wash of colour ran up her cheeks but she met his eyes. 'It could prove to be a strain, Dylan, couldn't it? D'you think we can handle a trip like this without it causing us both a great deal of…well, heartache?'

'Yes,' he said huskily, hoping and praying that he wasn't being overly optimistic. Maybe Joanna was fairly confident about her own self-control but could he handle being with her, day and night, for the duration of the conference?

His heart began singing that aria, trilling away so loudly that he had trouble hearing himself think, but this was too important to him to make a mistake at this stage. Even if he suffered the tortures of the damned he needed to have this time with her.

'I'm sure we can handle it, Joanna, the same as we've handled the past few weeks.' He shrugged, aiming for an air of nonchalance and obviously succeeding when she didn't disagree. He hurried on, taking advantage of her receptive mood.

'We're both adults and we both know the score. We can't get involved with one another so we just have to get on with the job. That's it, basically.'

Joanna managed not to betray any emotion but Dylan's calm assessment of the situation had made it sound as though he no longer cared that they could only ever be colleagues. Had he got over his attraction to her, then? Was that why they had managed so well to maintain a professional front throughout the past few weeks?

Her mind raced back over what had happened since they'd had breakfast together that January morning. Apart from that minor hiccup a few weeks ago when she'd been jealous about him talking to Sarah Rothwell, they had managed to keep things on a very even keel—so even, in fact, that it smacked of indifference rather than self-control. Could it be because Dylan had found someone else, another woman to occupy his thoughts, perhaps?

Her heart said no, it wasn't possible, but the calm way he was looking at her said that it was true. He had got over his *crush* on her and saw her now as just another colleague. It should have been reassuring to realise that, but it hurt too much to know that another woman had replaced her in his affections to derive any satisfaction from it.

'Then there's no need for us to worry, is there?' She summoned a smile as she jotted some notes on a memo slip, desperate not to make a fool of herself by breaking down. 'This is the date of the conference. It's the first weekend in April and we'll be in Paris from the Friday afternoon until Monday lunchtime. Diane is due back at work that week so she will keep everything ticking over in our absence.'

She passed him the memo as he came over to her desk. 'Brian will let you have all the details about our hotel, etc., but you may need to let people know that you'll be away that weekend.'

'Thanks.' He glanced at the paper and she wondered if it was her imagination that his hands seemed to be trembling.

She chased away that fanciful notion as he went

back to the door because it was ridiculous. Dylan was perfectly happy with the arrangements and didn't feel it would be a problem to go to Paris with her, so that was the end of the matter. Once he had told those people in his life who mattered what was happening it would be fine.

The thought of exactly who Dylan might need to tell about the forthcoming trip, however, wouldn't go away for the rest of the day. Despite how busy she was, Joanna thought about it almost continuously. She went home that night and set to work on the paper she would present at the conference as soon as she'd finished dinner but it was difficult to remember all the salient points she wanted to make when she kept trying to picture the woman who had captured Dylan's heart.

Was she blonde or brunette, tall or short, plump or slim? Where had he met her and how soon after they'd breakfasted together had he started dating her?

Joanna chewed the end of her pen as the questions ran through her head. Was she older than him or younger? Probably younger, she decided with a sinking heart, because most men preferred to date women who were younger than themselves.

That thought was even more disheartening. She got up and went to the window so she could look out across the rooftops of London. She had achieved all her dreams yet as she stood there, staring at the city, she couldn't help wishing that she'd met Dylan when she'd been starting out on her career. The outcome might have been very, very different if she had.

Charles de Gaulle airport was on high alert because of recent terrorist activities. Consequently, they were delayed while their luggage was searched by Customs.

Dylan unzipped his suit carrier then glanced over at Joanna who was at the neighbouring desk. She was busily repacking her case now that it had been checked and didn't appear to notice him looking at her although maybe that was just a cover. She'd been so very distant towards him in the past few weeks that he knew it had been deliberate even though he had no idea what he'd done to warrant such treatment. They'd seemed to be getting on so well before the trip to Paris had been mentioned, but he had noticed a marked change in her attitude towards him ever since then and the situation had gone from bad to worse that day.

Joanna had barely said a dozen words to him on the flight from Heathrow, making it clear that she hadn't wanted to chat by working on the paper she intended to present the following day. If she'd hung a placard round her neck with the words 'Don't Touch!' printed on it she couldn't have made her feelings any more clear, he thought wryly, yet why was she behaving this way? Was she worried in case he tried to make a play for her once they arrived on foreign soil?

Dylan's mouth thinned as he swung the suit carrier over his shoulder. He had never forced his attentions on a woman and he didn't intend to start doing so now! He waited until Joanna had finished repacking her bag then took her arm and briskly steered her out of the customs area, pausing only when they came to a quiet spot close to the restrooms.

'I think we need to get a few things straight before we go any further.' He didn't attempt to keep the bite out of his voice and he saw her head tilt back as though she was preparing for a fight. A thin smile curled his mouth because if she wanted to make an issue out of this then he was more than happy to oblige.

'I see.'

'No, I don't think you do see. That's the problem. I have no intention of *forcing* myself on you if that's what is worrying you, Joanna.' He laughed scathingly, wishing he didn't feel like such a louse when she paled. He didn't want to fight with her or hurt her— heaven forbid, it was the last thing he wanted to do! Nevertheless, he had to make it clear that she—and her virtue—were perfectly safe.

'It may surprise to you to learn that I have never, *ever* needed to use force with a woman.'

'I'm sure you haven't, Dr Archer. I'm sure that most women are only too happy to comply with your requests.'

Her head tilted back that bit further until she was positively staring down her elegant nose at him. However, Dylan had seen the hurt that had clouded her grey eyes and knew that his words had hit home far harder than he'd intended them to. He was suddenly torn by the need to apologise to her and at the same time make sure she understood that she was in no danger, but she didn't give him the chance to do either.

'Now, although this conversation is all very interesting, it would be far better if we made our way to our hotel and checked in. The welcome meeting is scheduled for two-thirty and we'll need to register beforehand.' Her delicate brows arched. 'Would you care to find us a taxi or shall I do it?'

'It's already arranged,' he explained shortly, turning

to lead the way to the exit. 'I booked a taxi to meet us here and take us to our hotel.'

'Oh. Right. I see. Th-thank you.'

The quaver in her voice caught him unawares because it was the first hint of weakness she'd betrayed in weeks. Dylan felt his anger melt away when he saw how uncertain she looked all of a sudden. Had it all been an act? he wondered. Was she really as indifferent to him as she'd pretended to be?

His spirits lifted even though he had nothing on which to base that assumption. The thought that Joanna might have been fighting her feelings by keeping him at arm's length cast a whole new light on the situation. He took a deep breath as they made their way across the arrivals hall. If nothing else happened this weekend he was going to find out how Joanna really felt about him...one way or the other.

'*Merci.*'

Joanna handed the taxi driver her case and got into the back of the cab. Dylan was making sure the driver knew where they were staying and it gave her a few precious moments to gather her composure.

The past few weeks had been such a strain. Keeping Dylan at a distance should have been easy enough, but it had proved far more difficult than she'd anticipated when each time she saw him she suffered an actual physical reaction. Leaping hearts and pounding pulses might be all well and good in a romance novel but they played havoc when one was trying to focus on lifesaving surgery. She'd felt completely wrung out each night after she'd left work and the fact that she'd had to face a repeat the following day had made life even more difficult. It made her wonder once again how she was going to get through this weekend. All she could do was to try and remember that Dylan was no longer interested in her and hope that it would help.

'The driver says it should take roughly half an hour to get to the hotel,' Dylan informed her as he climbed into the cab and slammed the door.

'Fine.' Joanna checked her watch, making herself think solely about their schedule. 'That will give us another half an hour to check in and get to the conference centre.'

'Thank heavens it's next to the hotel,' Dylan sighed, sinking back into the seat as the cab set off.

Joanna shot him a careful look from under her lashes and frowned when she realised how tired he looked. He looked as though he, too, had suffered a few sleepless nights of late.

Her heart plummeted because there was only one reason she could think of why Dylan might not have had enough sleep of late, and she didn't want to go there. No way! However, now the thought had entered her head it was impossible to chase it away.

Had he spent those nights with the new woman in his life?

Her stomach churned at the thought of him making love to another woman. It was so painful that she could hardly bear it, but she had to face up to the facts. Dylan was free to sleep with whoever he chose and there wasn't a thing she could do about it.

Silence fell inside the cab as it whizzed them into the centre of Paris. The traffic was a nightmare and she closed her eyes as they circled the Arc de Triomphe. If there was a system about who had priority then it certainly wasn't apparent. She was deeply relieved when the cab drew up outside their hotel and she could get out. She lifted her case out of the boot while Dylan dealt with the fare and made her way into the hotel. A bellboy took her bag then ushered her to the reception desk where she checked in. By the time she was handed a key to her room Dylan had arrived at the desk, but she paused only long enough to tell him that she would meet him back in the foyer in fifteen minutes' time before she hurried away. She may as well start the weekend as she meant to go on.

Her room was airy and spacious, the double-glazed windows affording her a wonderful view across the Champs Élysées to the River Seine. At any other time Joanna would have been delighted with her accommodation but it did little to lift her downbeat mood. Leaving her case on the stand to unpack later, she went into the bathroom and tidied her hair before setting off to the foyer to meet Dylan. She was just closing her bedroom door when the door to the adjoining room opened and Dylan appeared.

'Seems we're next to each other,' he remarked, tucking the key card into his suit pocket.

'Um…yes.' Joanna dredged up a sickly smile as she set off along the corridor as though pursued by demons. She could hear the sound of Dylan's footsteps following her and felt her throat close up with a sudden attack of nerves.

Why hadn't she given any thought to the fact that they might have adjoining bedrooms? If she'd been more on the ball she would have made a point of asking for a room on a different floor. Now the thought of lying in bed, knowing that Dylan was sleeping on the other side the wall, made her feel all hot and bothered, and it was just so ridiculous to let it upset her so much that she groaned out loud.

'Joanna? Are you all right?'

Dylan stopped her by dint of a hand on her arm and Joanna took a deep breath. She had to stop this and she had to stop it now, otherwise the next few days would be a living hell. If Dylan could cope with the situation then she could, too. She had to. It was as simple as that.

'I was just trying to remember if I'd brought all the conference bumph with me.' She opened her shoulder-bag and made a great production out of checking the wad of papers that had been sent by the conference organisers. 'They've made a big to-do about the fact that we need to have all the proper paperwork with us, otherwise we won't be allowed into the hall.'

'Looks as though it's all there from what I can see, but if you want to check then I can always run back and fetch anything you've forgotten.'

His kindness was almost her undoing and she had to blink hard to clear away the foolish tears that filled her eyes. 'No, I'm sure I've got everything I need. Anyway, you can always vouch for me if there's a problem, can't you?'

'Of course. I'd be happy to.'

There was an undercurrent in his voice which she might not have noticed if she hadn't been so attuned to him. Joanna felt a tremor work its way along her limbs until it reached the very centre of her chest where it turned into a glow of heat. She took a shaky breath but there was no way that she could keep the emotion out of her own voice no matter how hard she tried. 'Thank you.'

Dylan didn't say anything so she had no idea if he'd noticed her reaction or not. However, it was a relief when they carried on and reached the lifts. They stepped inside and Dylan pressed the button for the ground floor then smiled in delight as he glanced over his shoulder.

'Wow! What a fantastic view.'

Joanna looked round and suddenly realised that one wall of the lift was made entirely of glass. Through it she could see Paris laid out before her as they descended—the Grand Palais, the Eiffel Tower, the beautiful old buildings with their steep roofs and garrets. It was a beautiful day and the whole scene was backdropped by a clear blue sky, making her gasp with pleasure.

'That is so beautiful!'

'Isn't it just? Think we'll have time to do some sightseeing?'

'I hope so,' she replied without thinking then felt her heart lurch when she realised how dangerous it would be to wander the streets of Paris with Dylan.

She turned round when the lift came to a halt as they reached the foyer, fighting against the pictures that were gathering in her mind. She mustn't think about them walking hand in hand beside the Seine, stopping to kiss under the many bridges, neither must she think about them standing at the top of the Eiffel Tower and drinking in the view together. Paris might be a city for lovers but they weren't lovers—they were colleagues. She had to keep that at the forefront of her mind and use it to block out such nonsense. If it didn't work then she should remember the other woman in Dylan's life, the one who'd caused those dark circles under his eyes.

Her heart spasmed with a pain so sharp that it

seemed to pierce right through her soul. If Dylan could have chosen who he'd wanted to spend this weekend in Paris with she doubted if he would have chosen to spend it with *her*!

CHAPTER EIGHT

THIS was driving him crazy!

Dylan accepted another canapé from the waiter, tried again to focus on what was happening. The group he was currently with was discussing some new ground-breaking developments in post-operative care. Normally, he would have been eagerly storing up what he was hearing for later use, but he just couldn't seem to concentrate when he kept wondering what Joanna was doing.

Soft laughter suddenly flowed across the room and the hair on the back of his neck lifted in atavistic response. Red alert, his cells were screaming. Joanna's laughing. Prepare!

He glanced over his shoulder and felt his facial muscles go into spasm when he saw her smiling at a tall, distinguished-looking man whom he knew to be one of France's leading surgeons. There was no doubt at all that she and Jean-Pierre Duteil were getting along famously and a rush of jealousy hit him. He wanted to go straight over there and warn the other guy off, only he *knew* how Joanna would react if he did that.

He made himself take a couple of deep breaths before he turned back to the group once more. Some of the world's most distinguished surgeons were attending this conference and he'd be a fool to blot his copy book by appearing uninterested in what was going on. Who knew where he could end up working if the situation between him and Joanna grew too fraught to handle?

The welcome party finally came to an end and people started to leave to go back to their hotels. There was a formal dinner being held that evening and it was obvious that everyone was eager to take a break beforehand. Dylan made his way across the room to where Joanna was still deep in conversation with Jean-Pierre Duteil. She didn't appear to have noticed him so it gave him a chance to study the couple's body language from close quarters and, quite frankly, he didn't like what he saw. Duteil was giving out some very strong signals indeed.

'Sorry to interrupt, Joanna, but I'm heading back to the hotel now.'

He ruthlessly cut into the conversation before Duteil could reply. He saw the Frenchman glance at him and threw caution to the winds as he returned the look with one which must have left Duteil in little doubt about his feelings. To hell with *entente cordiale*—this was war!

'Fine. I'll be along shortly.' Joanna seemed oblivious to the undercurrents as she treated Dylan to a coolly dismissive smile. Her expression warmed up several degrees, however, when she turned to the Frenchman again and Dylan ground his teeth. Maybe he was in danger of making a fool of himself but there was no way that he was prepared to leave her here.

'I was hoping you would go over some notes with me,' he insisted, neatly positioning himself between her and the other man. 'It's almost five now so there isn't much time before we need to get ready for dinner. I'd like to be sure I've covered all the points I wanted to make when I present my paper tomorrow.'

'I'm sure your paper will be perfectly fine,' she said, even more coldly.

'I'd still appreciate your input if you could spare the time,' he shot back.

'I can see that you two have much to discuss. I, too, need to check my notes for the speech I shall be making after dinner tonight.' Jean-Pierre's expression was bland as he lifted Joanna's hand to his lips and kissed it with Gallic panache. '*A bientôt*, Joanna. I look forward to seeing you again tonight. You, too, Dr Archer, of course.'

Dylan inclined his head but if Duteil hadn't had the sense to leave then he'd have had no hesitation about suggesting it. Joanna glared at him as soon as the Frenchman was safely out of earshot.

'What *do* you think you're doing? That was so rude! You made it perfectly plain just now that you wanted Jean-Pierre to leave.'

'Good! At least I achieved something. And if it also saved you from making a fool of yourself then that's another brownie point I've just earned for myself.'

He swung round and strode to the exit, leaving Joanna to follow him if that was what she chose to do. It was, but it didn't mean that she wasn't furious about what had happened.

'Making a fool of myself? What the hell do you mean by that?'

'I should have thought it was obvious,' he snapped, exiting the conference centre to go back to their hotel. It was the evening rush hour and the street was crowded with people leaving work. Many were making for the pavement cafés which lined the road to enjoy a glass of wine before they returned home. Dylan was sorely tempted to join them only alcohol wouldn't cure his problems. Joanna couldn't give a damn about him—that was obvious from the way she had been making sheep's eyes at Duteil all afternoon. The thought might have brought him to his knees if he hadn't been so furious.

'Maybe it was obvious to you but it certainly isn't obvious to me.' She grabbed his arm and hung on when he carried on walking, forcing him either to stop or run the risk of pulling her over.

'What did you mean, Dylan? I want to know,' she demanded when he halted.

'That you and Duteil made it perfectly obvious that you had other thoughts on your mind rather than the joys of surgery.'

His smile was deliberately offensive even though he hated himself for behaving this way with her. He'd wanted this weekend to be a time to cherish, something he could look back on when the ache in his heart grew too painful to bear. He'd hoped to store it all up—minute by minute, hour by hour, day by day— yet here he was, standing on the streets of Paris hurling *insults* at her.

He ran a hand over his face as the sheer enormity of what he was doing hit him squarely in the chest with a massive thump. 'I'm sorry, Joanna,' he said hoarsely, wondering if she could tell how wretched he felt. Was it any wonder she had responded to Duteil with all flags flying when *he* behaved like such an arrogant boor?

'And so you should be. For your information, Jean-Pierre and I were discussing a new microsurgical technique which his clinic is developing. He offered to demonstrate it to me if we can arrange a time and a date that suits us both.'

'Great. I'm sure you'll enjoy it,' he agreed flatly, his self-esteem sinking even lower into the mud. *Squelch.*

'I'm sure I shall. I'm sure you will, too, because I suggested to Jean-Pierre that you might like to observe the technique as well.' She took a quick breath but he heard the strain in her voice when she continued.

'That's all we were discussing, Dylan. Work. That's why I came to this conference and why I thought you came, too. Maybe I was wrong about that, as I might have been wrong about a lot of other things of late, it seems.'

'What sort of other things?' he asked numbly, struggling to keep his head above the tide of relief that was swirling around him. Did Joanna mean that she wasn't interested in Duteil, or at least not *that* way?

The waves washed right over his head at that point so that he missed her reply. 'I'm sorry. What did you say?'

'I *asked* if you had a girlfriend,' she repeated, with more than a touch of asperity in her voice this time.

'A girlfriend?'

'Yes.' She rolled her eyes. 'Why do men have to make life so complicated by repeating everything one says?'

'Probably because they're afraid they might not have heard you correctly the first time and don't want to jump in feet first and make a complete mess of things.'

'Well, for your information, you did hear me correctly. So if you'd care to answer my question some time in the *not-too-distant* future maybe we can get on with the rest of the evening!'

'Far be it from me to spoil our evening, Joanna,' he

said silkily, loving the way she immediately blushed and lowered her eyes. He took a steadying breath, not wanting to do what he'd been so keen to avoid—jump in feet first and trample down this tiny bud of hope that had started sprouting.

It was his turn now to roll his eyes when he realised how fanciful he was getting. Time to get those feet firmly back on the ground, Archer, he told himself sternly.

He turned to face her, wanting to see her expression when he gave her the answer she had demanded. Maybe it was silly to hope it would mean something— *really* mean something—to her, but what did he have to lose?

'No. I don't have a girlfriend. I haven't even asked anyone out since that day we had breakfast together.' He shrugged. 'There was no point.'

'No point?'

The breathy note in her voice was like music to his ears and balm to his soul and all sorts of other poetic things to various parts of his anatomy he wasn't going to think about right then. He took her hands—both of them—and kissed them with very little finesse but a whole ton of emotion.

'There's no point asking another woman out when I'm only interested in you.'

Joanna felt the relief rush to the top of her head and down to the tips of her toes. It was the strangest and yet the most wonderful feeling she had ever known. She gripped Dylan's hands, wanting him to know how much it meant to her that he hadn't found someone else. Maybe it was silly to feel like this and maybe she would regret it later, but she was only human.

Discovering there wasn't another woman in his life or his affections meant the world to her.

'I'm glad. I thought that you must have found someone else,' she said honestly, because it was way too difficult to lie just to keep face.

'No. I haven't even looked for anyone because I'm not interested.' He rubbed his thumbs over her knuckles and her knees threatened to buckle when she felt desire pouring through her in a hot, melting tide.

'I think we both need to sit down for a moment, don't you?' The rough note in his voice told her that he was feeling just as shaky as she was so she didn't protest when he led her to one of the pavement cafés. He pulled out a chair for her then sat down beside her, and she smiled when she heard him let out a huge sigh.

'What was that for?'

'Relief.' He looked at her and grinned sheepishly. 'For a horrible moment back there I honestly and truly thought my legs were going to give way!'

'Me, too,' she admitted, loving the way his green eyes seemed to be lit by an inner glow as he looked at her. When he leant over and kissed her gently on the mouth she didn't draw back, couldn't have done because she needed this kiss to survive, every bit as much as she needed food or oxygen.

A tremor shot through her because she'd never admitted to herself until that moment just how important Dylan was to her. She needed to see him and speak to him just so she could function properly, and the thought of how dependent she had become on him scared her. It was a relief when the waiter arrived to take their order because it gave her a breathing space. Dylan ordered wine for them both and she couldn't

even be bothered to protest because he hadn't consulted her first. It just seemed to highlight the effect
he had on her. She had never allowed a man to make
decisions for her, mainly because she'd had such a
hard struggle to prove herself throughout her career,
yet it didn't seem to matter if Dylan took control. In
a funny kind of a way that scared her even more because she *should* be afraid of losing her independence.

'Don't!'

She looked up when he touched her hand and there
was no way that she could hide her fears when she
saw the concern in his eyes. 'I'm scared, Dylan. I
don't know what I'm getting into or even if it's what
I want.'

'I know. And I wish to heaven that I knew how to
make you understand that everything will work out but
I don't.' He squeezed her fingers and she could tell
that he was desperate to convince her. 'I know you
have doubts, Joanna. I think you're wrong to put so
much emphasis on the negative points of us having a
relationship but that's just my feelings on the matter.
I can't feel the way you do even though I desperately
want to. I can only try to understand and reassure you,
and I'm terrified that it won't be enough.'

Her eyes filled with tears at his kindness and com-
passion. 'And I can't promise you that your reassur-
ances will work either, so if you want to call a halt
now I'll understand.'

'No. Even if this lasts just as long as the weekend
does I don't want to stop.'

His tone was fierce all of a sudden and she smiled.
'It's difficult to argue with that.'

'Good! That's what I was hoping.' His mouth curled
up at the corners as he smiled into her eyes. 'Obvi-

ously, it pays to play the macho male when the situation warrants it.'

'So long as you don't hit me over the head with a club and then drag me back to your cave,' she retorted.

'No way. Cross my heart, etcetera. My plan is a little more subtle than that.'

'Oh, so you have a plan, do you? Did you have this all worked out before we set off this morning?'

'No. I'm just very adaptable and think on my feet,' he assured her, chuckling.

The waiter arrived with their wine and she waited until he'd gone before answering. 'All right. I'll give you the benefit of the doubt and accept that you didn't have this all planned out. So, that being the case, what have you in mind?'

'First of all we'll go back to our hotel and change for dinner. Even though I could think of a dozen better ways to spend our first evening in Paris, duty calls. With a bit of luck, dinner should be over by ten so the rest of the night will be ours to do with as we choose.'

'Sounds promising,' she murmured, watching him over the rim of the glass as she took a sip of wine.

'Oh, I think I can guarantee that you won't be disappointed. After all, it will be the first chance we have to spend any real, quality time together away from work.' His tone was husky as he picked up his glass and chinked it against hers. 'Here's to us and Paris…the city of lovers.'

'To us and Paris,' she repeated, knowing exactly what he'd meant even though he hadn't actually come out and said the words.

Her breath caught because by tomorrow they would be lovers, she and Dylan. Even though she knew the problems still hadn't been resolved, she didn't have any doubts that it was what she wanted. She would worry about the future after they returned from Paris but for now this weekend would be theirs.

Dylan could barely wait for dinner to end. He and Joanna had been seated next to each other and every time he moved he could feel his arm brushing hers or their thighs touching. It was like being put through the torments of the damned, but all he could do was to grit his teeth and think about what was to come.

He gulped a mouthful of coffee and just managed to stop himself choking when the hot liquid shot down his throat. Thinking about what might happen later that evening did very little for his equilibrium. He turned when the woman on his left asked him a question and for the rest of the meal concentrated on behaving like a guest at an Emily Post dinner party would have done. Nobody could have faulted his manners or his attention level although maybe he went a bit too far because it was obvious the middle-aged brunette had got the entirely wrong idea. It was a relief for a number of reasons when dinner came to an end and he could make his escape.

He stood up, politely refusing the brunette's invitation to join her in the bar for a brandy with what he hoped was a suitable amount of regret. Joanna was speaking to the man who'd been seated on her right and Dylan waited while they finished their conversation. He took her arm as soon as the other man had departed and bustled her towards the door.

'What's the rush?' she asked, coquettishly batting her eyelashes at him.

'If I don't get you somewhere quiet I'm very much

afraid that we might cause a scene,' he growled, unable even to pretend to play games.

'Oh!'

A tide of colour ran up her cheeks and he chuckled as he backed her into a handy alcove and kissed her quickly on the lips. 'Oh, indeed.'

They carried on across the foyer, pausing only long enough to collect their coats. Several people wished them goodnight but, thankfully, nobody tried to stop them so that within minutes they found themselves out in the street. It was a beautiful night, a tiny breeze ruffling the tops of the trees on the Champs Élysées, the ink-black sky sprinkled with stars. By tacit consent they headed towards the river and Dylan took Joanna's hand as they walked down the steps to the embankment and strolled along beside the water until they came to the Pont Neuf.

Dylan stopped in the shadows beneath the beautiful old bridge and took Joanna into his arms, overwhelmed with relief that he was finally able to hold her. Sitting next to her at dinner had simply increased his hunger for her, but he didn't want to rush her...

She wound her arms around his neck, pulled his head down so she could fit her mouth to his and all thoughts of restraint fled in an instant. If he was hungry for the feel and taste of her then Joanna was just as hungry for him.

Their mouths brushed, clung then parted, their breath coming in laboured spurts as passion rose and filled them with an elemental need for satisfaction. Dylan framed her face between his hands, feeling every scrap of his being aching as he looked at her. She was so beautiful as she stood there in the shadow of the bridge, her face softly lit by starlight. Her eyes

were closed and her lips were parted and he knew that
he would remember this moment when he was old and
grey and other memories had faded into the mists of
time. He loved her so much and he longed to tell her
that, but he knew it would be overstepping the last
boundary and that she wasn't ready for it. Not yet. He
had to show her with deeds, not words, how he felt
and pray that she would let herself respond with her
heart, not her head.

He kissed her again, softly and with a tenderness
that stemmed from love, then took hold of her hand
again. They started walking back the way they'd come
and once again they didn't speak. The hotel foyer was
crowded when they passed through it—a lot of the
delegates from the conference had booked rooms there
because it was so convenient. However, they didn't
stop to speak to anyone as they went straight to the
lift.

They got out at their floor and walked along the
corridor together, stopping when they reached their
rooms. Dylan turned to her and smiled, knowing that
he was about to embark on something so momentous
that his life would be forever changed afterwards.

'My room or yours?'

'It doesn't matter,' she said huskily, looking up at
him with a wealth of emotion in her eyes.

'You're right. It doesn't.'

He bent and kissed her, kept on kissing her as he
somehow managed to unlock the door and get them
both inside his room. Bending, he lifted her into his
arms and carried her across to the bed, placing her
gently on the quilted satin cover before kneeling beside her so he could kiss her cheeks, her chin, the tip
of her elegant nose, the arch of her silky brows. Her

skin was warm and smooth, her long lashes tickling his mouth as he dropped kisses on her eyelids, making him smile for joy. He loved every bit of her that he'd seen so far and it could only get better!

Joanna didn't stop him as he unbuttoned the jacket of her black silk suit. She was wearing just a black lace bra beneath it and he had to pause for a second because the sight of her full breasts encased by the delicate lace was too wonderful not to savour.

He slid the jacket off her shoulders and hung it carefully over the back of a chair then unzipped her skirt and slid it off—inch by delicious inch—revealing her hips, her gently rounded stomach, her slender thighs...

His breath caught and he couldn't breathe in or out when he discovered that she was wearing stockings and suspenders. The garter belt matched her black lace panties and it seemed such a sexy garment for her to wear that he was momentarily stunned. It was only when she shifted restlessly that he managed to stir himself into action again, although maybe he would need to calm himself down a little before he went any further, he decided when he felt his body respond with enthusiastic fervour to the sight of her.

He stood up and draped her skirt over the chair, hoping to give himself time to gather his composure, but the moment he turned and saw her lying there on the bed he went weak at the knees and rigid in other places.

He sat down beside her and smoothed back her hair with hands that trembled. He'd made love to his fair share of women in the past but this was so different that it didn't even bear comparison. What if he wasn't up to the job? What if he disappointed her? What if...?

She slid her hands up his chest and tugged at the

ends of his bowtie so that it unravelled, and every single rational thought fled. The tiny onyx shirt-studs which had caused him so much grief when he'd been getting ready that night popped out of their button-holes as if by magic under her dextrous fingers. Dylan gritted his teeth when he felt her hands slide inside the open shirt-front and start exploring. Joanna had surgeon's hands—strong palms and supple fingers—and she used them to full advantage as she smoothed and stroked and caressed him until he was in such a state he could barely remember his own name.

He ripped the shirt off his back and tossed it into the corner before he lay down beside her. 'Do you have any idea what you're doing to me, you wicked woman?'

'Yes.' The laughter in her eyes was like a wonderful gift, easing away any last doubts he'd had about what they were doing and the effects it could have on her later. Joanna hadn't been coerced into letting this hap-pen—she was a willing participant. More than willing, he amended when he felt her hand searching for the zip on his trousers.

He kissed her deeply, his tongue sliding into the sweet recesses of her mouth while her searching hand found and caressed him. His body was pulsing with need now, demanding a release, but he was determined to hold back until he was sure she was ready.

He rolled onto his back, taking her with him so that she was suddenly lying on top of him, her weight pressing down on him, her body in the most intimate contact with his own. It took just a moment to free her breasts from the lacy cups of the bra, another moment before she gasped as he suckled her nipples, a few seconds more before he felt her moving against him, but even then he held back. He wanted this night to be the most wonderful experience of her life and he would wait until the time was right even if it killed him!

'Dylan!'

She moaned his name out loud as passion built inside her and reached unbearable levels. Dylan quickly rolled over again then stood up and removed the rest of his clothes. Her skin was burning hot when he went back to her, lightly filmed with perspiration so that he could taste the moisture on his lips as he skimmed kisses from her throat to her thighs before he finally settled over her. Their joining was so swift and easy that he laughed in delight, loving the way they fitted together so perfectly that they might have been made for each other. It made their love-making seem even more special, even more right.

'Love me, Dylan,' she whispered, her arms clinging to him, her legs wrapping around him.

'I shall,' he whispered back in the instant before passion claimed him and speech became impossible. But even though he could no longer say the words out loud he could hear them in his head and in his heart.

He loved her and he would always love her—from now until eternity.

CHAPTER NINE

PALE fingers of light filtered into the room and Joanna stirred. She felt so warm and comfortable that she really didn't want to get up. She burrowed deeper into the pillow, only instead of cool, crisp cotton her cheek encountered the warmth and smoothness of bare skin.

Her eyes flew open and her heart missed a beat when she found herself staring at Dylan. His eyes were wide open and it looked as though he'd been awake for some time. Had he been lying there, watching her, while she'd been sleeping? The thought was so intimate that a shiver raced through her and she saw him frown.

'You're not cold, are you, darling?' he asked, drawing her closer against him.

'No,' she murmured, wondering if anything had ever felt as marvellous as it did to be held like this. She felt so safe and secure, so wonderfully *cherished*, that tears of happiness prickled her eyes.

'Hey, what's the matter? You're not sorry about what happened last night, are you?'

The concern in his voice would have been balm to her soul if it had needed any solace. However, her soul and the rest of her seemed to be in excellent shape that morning. She smiled as she blinked away the tears.

'No, I'm not sorry. I'm just being a typical woman and coming over all emotional because I never thought I could feel like this.'

'That's a relief!' He rewarded her with a kiss. 'So it wasn't too bad, then?'

'Fishing for compliments, Dr Archer?'

'Of course not,' he denied, but she saw the rim of colour that ran along his cheekbones and her heart overflowed with tenderness and all sorts of other emotions she didn't dare examine too closely whilst she was so vulnerable. It would be easy to let herself believe that she'd fallen in love with him, but it would create far too many problems to allow that to happen.

'Good, because there's no need to fish,' she said, deliberately putting the thought out of her mind because she didn't want anything to spoil their happiness. 'It was the most wonderful night of my entire life, Dylan, and I shall never forget it.'

'High praise indeed.' Sadness flickered in his eyes despite the fact that he smiled at her. Joanna frowned when he tossed back the quilt and stood up.

'What did I say?' She reached over and caught his hand, gently tugging him back down onto the bed beside her. 'Dylan, what's wrong?'

'Nothing.' He touched the tip of her nose with his finger and his eyes were very grave all of a sudden. 'Last night was the most wonderful night of my life, too, Joanna.'

He drew her to him and kissed her with a passion that soon had her clinging to him, but even through the heat of their desire the nagging doubt that something was troubling him refused to budge. Was it the fact that she'd not tried to pretend their relationship would continue once the weekend was over, perhaps?

Her heart ached because she sensed it was so and she hated to think that she had hurt him. However, it would be wrong to lie and terribly wrong to make promises she couldn't keep. All she could do was to show him how much she valued what they had at that moment, and she did. She did!

Their love-making seemed to reach new heights, as though both of them needed to prove to each other how special it was. Joanna lay back against the pillows afterwards while Dylan went to take a shower, wishing that she could feel this way for ever, but it just wasn't possible. Making a commitment to Dylan was out of the question yet she knew in her heart that the alternative—suggesting they should have an affair—wouldn't be enough for either of them. They would start to want more than that, to want things they could never have. It would be far, far better if they enjoyed this one weekend together and settled for that, but could they go back to being simply colleagues after it was over?

Dylan turned the thermostat on the shower to cold and made himself stand under the icy jets until his skin was puckered with goose-pimples. Turning off the water, he reached for a towel and dried himself off then unhooked the robe from the back of the door. He tightened the belt and took a deep breath before opening the bathroom door.

He refused to spoil the weekend by thinking about the future. It wouldn't be easy because that remark Joanna had made about remembering last night for the rest of her life had struck home far harder than it should have done. He'd known from the outset that they would only have these few days together but somewhere along the way—probably in the aftermath of their love-making last night—he'd allowed himself to hope they could have more than that. Now he had to get his feet back onto the ground and not make the mistake of ruining what precious time they had left.

'I don't know about you but I'm starving. How about if I ring for room service and ask them to bring us some breakfast?' he suggested, adopting a deliberately upbeat tone as he went back into the bedroom.

'Sounds good to me… Wait a minute, though. Wasn't there something on the conference agenda about a breakfast meeting this morning?' She frowned as she looked around the room. 'Where did I put my bag? I'm sure I've got all the details in it.'

'Do you really want to start the day by discussing work when you could be enjoying this view?' He pushed the heavy satin drapes aside so that the morning sunlight spilled into the room. 'We've got the rest of the weekend to work so surely it won't hurt if we play truant for a couple of hours?'

'I don't suppose it would matter that much,' she conceded. 'Anyway, from what I remember, it's supposed to be more of a social event than a proper working breakfast.'

'Well, I, for one, would far rather socialise with you than the rest of the crowd. Why don't you have a shower while I rustle up some food?' He briskly swept the voile curtains aside as well and grinned. 'I can guarantee this view will blow you away!'

'So long as it doesn't blow me that far away that I'm unable to present my paper this morning,' she retorted, tossing back the quilt. 'I really don't want to make a complete fool of myself.'

'There's very little danger of that happening. But if there is a problem I can always administer a bit of timely first aid.'

He went over to the bed and pulled her into his

arms, feeling his body stir to life when his hands encountered bare skin. It was an effort to let her go after he'd kissed when what he *really* wanted to do was to make love to her again. He could have happily spent the whole day in bed with her, in fact, but his conscience would give him hell if he didn't do what he was being paid to do and attend the conference. Having a highly developed sense of duty could be a real handicap at times!

Joanna disappeared into the bathroom while he phoned room service and ordered breakfast for them. He could hear the shower running when he hung up so he quickly got dressed. If he hurried he should have time to visit the florist's shop in the foyer before she finished in the bathroom.

By the time Joanna appeared ten minutes later Dylan had everything organised. He'd placed the table right in front of the window and stuck the rather wilting bunch of freesias he'd bought from the florist in a bottle of mineral water from the mini-bar and arranged it in the centre. He saw Joanna stop when she spotted them.

'Flowers! But where did they come from?'

'The shop in the foyer.' He grimaced. 'I'm afraid there wasn't much of a selection because they were waiting for a fresh delivery. I hope they're all right?'

'They're absolutely lovely! I adore freesias.' She went over to the table and bent down to sniff them. 'Thank you, Dylan. It was a really sweet thing to do. I can't remember the last time anyone bought me flowers.'

'It was my pleasure,' he said huskily, thinking that he would send her flowers every day of the week if it made her happy. He couldn't believe that she didn't get bombarded with them on a regular basis, in fact. She was so beautiful and talented that by rights she should have had men queuing up to lavish attention on her. It couldn't be for lack of offers, he decided, so it must be because she didn't encourage them, and that thought was both reassuring and at the same time worrying. Joanna was so determined to remain unattached that it just seemed to prove how foolish it would be to hope he could change her mind.

The waiter arrived with the breakfast trolley at that point, thankfully enough, so Dylan was able to put the thought to the back of his mind. He tipped the man then wheeled the trolley over to the table and pulled out a chair. 'Breakfast is served, *Madame*!'

'Thank you kindly.' Joanna sat down, laughing when he took a linen napkin off the trolley and draped it over her lap with a flourish. 'You seem to be rather good at this, if you don't mind my saying so.'

'I should be.' He picked up the ornate silver coffee-pot and filled their cups. 'I worked as a waiter to help pay my way through med school. I'm a whiz at the napkin-draping lark, and as for silver service... Well, you should just see me handling a spoon and a fork while I dish up veggies. It's sheer poetry in motion even though I say so myself.'

'Sounds like a treat not to be missed.' She chuckled as she took a warm croissant out of the basket. Breaking off an end, she popped it into her mouth.

'Any time you want a demonstration just say the word.' Dylan helped himself to a croissant and sat down. He broke off a chunk and spread it liberally with strawberry conserve before popping it into his mouth.

'I'll hold you to that.' She sipped some coffee then

looked at him curiously. 'So you had to work your way through university, did you? Your parents didn't support you?'

'Not financially. They didn't have the money to spare, but they gave me all the support I needed in other areas,' he explained. 'They were one hundred per cent behind me from the moment I told them I wanted to be a doctor and I'll always be grateful to them for that. I don't know if I'd have made it if they hadn't believed in me.'

'It helps if people encourage you to pursue your dreams,' she said rather wistfully.

'It does.' He put down his knife and looked at her. 'Weren't your parents keen on you going into medicine?'

'They didn't have an opinion one way or the other.' She shrugged when he frowned. 'They neither encouraged nor discouraged me because they considered it to be my decision.'

'That sounds very…well, *distant*, I suppose, is the word that springs to mind.'

'Actually, it's highly appropriate because they're very distant people. They were both heavily involved with their own careers whilst I was growing up. My father was a high court judge before he retired and my mother was a concert pianist. The live in Bermuda now so I see them only occasionally.'

'Do you miss them?' he put in quietly, not wanting her to stop there.

'Not really. I had a nanny until I was old enough to be sent away to boarding school. When I came home for the holidays, my parents were always working so I was looked after by our housekeeper. I expect that's why we've never been very close.'

'Just the opposite to me,' he said cheerfully, because he hated to hear that note of reserve in her voice. He couldn't imagine having parents like hers, ones who didn't take any interest in what their child was doing. 'We're still very close now, too. I have four sisters and we all try to get home to see Mum and Dad as often as we can.'

'I can't imagine what it's like, having sisters or brothers. I always had the impression that my parents hadn't planned on having any children and that I was an accident. It must have been fun growing up as part of a big family.'

'It was certainly hectic. I don't know how Mum used to cope but she never seemed to turn a hair and just got on with it. She's exactly the same now when we all go home for Christmas or family birthdays,' he explained, thinking how awful it must have been for Joanna as a child to feel that she hadn't been wanted. Maybe that explained why she tended to appear so aloof at times? It was an inbuilt defence mechanism to stop herself getting hurt.

The thought of her less than idyllic childhood touched him deeply but he knew better than to sympathise. He focused instead on recounting a very shortened version of his family history. 'My sisters are all older than me and they're all married with children. Would you believe that I'm an uncle nine times over? It's absolute bedlam when we all get together!'

'Good heavens!' she exclaimed. 'All those nephews and nieces must really keep you on your toes, Uncle Dylan.'

'They do, but I've always wanted a family of my own one day so it isn't a problem.'

'I'm sure it isn't.'

Once again there was a certain flatness to her voice. Dylan was tempted to ask her what was wrong but he managed to resist it. He swallowed a sigh because even though he desperately wanted to know everything possible about Joanna, there were still boundaries which he sensed she was unwilling to cross even after what had happened between them. It was frustrating to have to hold back when his instincts were to be open about his feelings, but he didn't want to make her feel guilty when this weekend ended. *She* had to want to take their relationship further and it wouldn't work if he tried to persuade her.

It was a sobering thought and too much to deal with right then. Even though he knew he could be storing up problems, he made himself put it aside. They finished their breakfast while they watched Paris waking up below them. Cars were flying down the Champs Élysées by the time they finished the last dregs of coffee and the pavements were full of commuters on their way to the Métro.

Dylan sighed as he put down his cup. 'Time we got ready and joined the fray, I suppose. What time is the first session scheduled?'

'Nine o'clock, I think.' Joanna got up and fetched her bag off the chest of drawers. She quickly consulted the programme and nodded. 'Yes, nine o'clock. Jean-Pierre and one of his colleagues are presenting a paper on this new microsurgical technique I was telling you about.'

'Should be exciting,' he replied with a marked lack of enthusiasm.

Her brows arched. 'Do you have something against Professor Duteil?'

'Nothing, apart from the fact that he's obviously smitten with you.'

She laughed throatily, a teasing sound that made his insides turn to jelly. 'If I didn't know better, Dylan Archer, I'd think you were jealous.'

He shrugged, not sure if he wanted to admit to such feelings. 'Really?'

'Yes, *really*.' She moved behind his chair and looped her arms around his neck. 'I think it's very sweet, Dylan. Really I do.'

Her tone mocked him but he probably deserved it for behaving like an idiot. She'd only been talking to the Frenchman, for pity's sake! It wasn't as though he'd caught them *in flagrante delicto*. Jealousy was for teenagers, not grown men who'd had enough experience of life—and women—to know better. But even after that little pep talk he couldn't have put his hand on his heart and sworn that he'd vanquished the green-eyed monster for good.

'There's no need to be jealous, you know.' She brushed his ear with her lips, her warm breath making him shiver when he felt it tickling his skin. Her mouth slid lower so she could deposit several more deliciously tempting kisses on his jaw. He'd not shaved yet that morning and he could feel the velvety softness of her lips snagging on the barbs of his beard and almost groaned out loud because of how it made him feel. It was just the thought of that teenager he seemed to be turning into—the one who was jealous and gauche and Lord knew what else—that helped him hang on.

'Isn't there?' he gritted out from between tightly clenched teeth.

'Of course not. Granted, Jean-Pierre is a very charming man and a talented surgeon, but my interest in him is purely professional, you understand.'

'I see. So do I take it, then, that your interest in me isn't just professional?' he asked, because he couldn't resist it.

'Not at the moment it isn't,' she admitted huskily.

Her mouth travelled down his neck, scattering kisses at random, and his throat moved convulsively as he swallowed down his next words. There was no point telling her that he wanted her feelings to last for longer than just this moment. It would only spoil what they had, and he wouldn't do that.

He pulled her down onto his lap and kissed her with every scrap of pent-up emotion he possessed. They had barely three days to make a lifetime of memories and he wasn't going to waste a second. Maybe they would go back to normal after that, but maybe, just maybe, she would think about what had happened this weekend and wonder if she was right to be so against them having a real relationship.

It was the dimmest ray of hope but it was something to hold onto in the dark.

Merci. Thank you.'

Joanna breathed out a sigh of relief as she sat down. Her paper had been well received and several people in the audience had asked some very in-depth questions afterwards. She glanced at Dylan and felt a little glow fill her when he smiled at her. She could tell that he had enjoyed her performance and it just seemed to put the seal on her pleasure. If Dylan approved then all was right with her world.

The thought was deeply disquieting because once again it made her see how much influence he had over her. Even before last night his views had mattered, and now they seemed to count for even more. Would they be able to resume their previous status when they got back to London? Or would it be too difficult to separate themselves from what had happened during this weekend?

The thought nagged away at her for the rest of the morning so that by the time they broke for lunch, she had a headache threatening. Dylan obviously guessed something was wrong because he drew her into a quiet corner.

'You look worn out, Joanna. Are you feeling all right?'

'I think I'm getting a headache,' she confessed, rubbing her throbbing temples.

'Do you want to go back to the hotel? There's just one more speech after lunch, I think.' He hunted the programme out of his pocket and nodded. 'Yes. One of the German delegates is talking about the problems of providing health care for the vast number of asylum-seekers who are flooding into Europe.'

'I particularly wanted to hear what he said,' Joanna explained. 'We're under a lot of pressure at St Leonard's—'

She got no further when a deafening explosion suddenly rocked the building. Chunks of plaster began to rain down from the ceiling and the room quickly filled with clouds of dust.

'Come along!' Dylan took her arm and briskly steered her to the exit. The other delegates were trying to leave so there was a small jam at the doors, but fortunately nobody seemed to be panicking. They made it outside eventually and stopped on the pavement. They could hear the sound of sirens as the police and emergency services rushed to the area, but it was difficult to tell what had happened.

'Wait here while I try and find out what's going on,' Dylan instructed tersely. He turned to hurry along the street to where a crowd had gathered around the entrance to the Métro, but Joanna caught hold of his sleeve.

'Be careful, won't you?'

'Don't worry. I shall.' He squeezed her hand then hurried away.

Joanna waited in the road, shaking her head when several people from the conference asked her if she knew what had happened. The police were starting to cordon off the area and she knew it wouldn't be long before she was told to leave. She didn't intend to go anywhere until she knew Dylan was all right, however, so when she spotted Jean-Pierre Duteil talking to one of the gendarmes she hurried over to him.

'What's happened?' she demanded as the policeman moved away.

'There has been an explosion on the Métro. The police think it may have been a bomb but they do not know for certain yet.'

'A bomb!' Joanna echoed in dismay. 'Are there many people injured?'

'Sadly, yes. The station was full apparently, and there was a train arriving when the explosion happened. I am going straight to Sancerre Hospital to await the injured.'

'Is there anything we can do to help?' she offered immediately. 'If there are a lot of casualties you'll need extra staff to help you. Dylan and I would like to be of use.'

'That would be wonderful, Joanna. *Merci*.' Jean-

Pierre took a card out of his top pocket and gave it to her. 'Here is the address of the hospital. I shall tell my staff to expect you.'

He hurried away and she saw him hailing a taxi. The police were making their way towards her and she knew it wouldn't be long before she had to move on. She scanned the crowd and breathed a sigh of relief when she saw Dylan making his way towards her.

'The police think it might have been a bomb but they're not sure. There's a lot of folk injured, though,' he told her.

'I know. I was just speaking to Jean-Pierre. He's gone back to his hospital and I told him that we'd like to help. Is that all right with you?' she added as an afterthought.

'Of course! Do you have the address?' He took the card then put his arm around her waist and led her away from the chaos. 'Let's find a cab and go straight there.'

It took them some time to find a taxi because there were a lot of people trying to get away from the scene of the incident, but finally they were on their way. Joanna had no idea what would greet them at the hospital but they would cope. Together.

Her heart filled with a bitter-sweet pain as the thought sank in. She could cope with anything so long as Dylan was beside her, but it would be a mistake to let herself become dependent on him.

'Fractured sternum which, from the look of this shadow, may have punctured the pericardium. There's definitely fluid accumulating around the heart so this one is top priority for surgery.'

Dylan removed the X-ray from the light-box while

the nurse who had been assigned to help him trans-
lated for her colleagues' benefit. He and Joanna had
been sent to the traumatology department as soon as
they had arrived at the hospital. As well as the main
theatres on one of the upper floors, there were also
two, small, well-equipped Theatres attached to the department. They had been in constant use ever since he
and Joanna had got there—in fact, Joanna was currently working in one of them, assisting one of the
hospital's own surgical team. Dylan would relieve her
once the operation was finished but in the meantime
he was making himself useful by doing triage.

The patient was rushed upstairs and the next trolley
was wheeled in. The waiting-area had been turned into
a holding bay for the injured. The nurse had told him
that the walking wounded were being seen at a local
clinic so the patients they were dealing with tended to
be the most badly injured. Fortunately, the staff had
set up an excellent system and were making sure that
everyone was X-rayed on admission. It made it much
easier for him to assess the extent of their injuries.
He'd just taken a fresh X-ray out of its folder when
Joanna appeared.

'Theatre's all yours. We've finished our stint now.'

Dylan quickly excused himself and drew her aside.
'How did it go?' He sighed when she shook her head.
'That bad, eh?'

'The poor girl had just stepped off the train when
the bomb went off, and she took the full brunt of the
explosion. There was very little we could do for her.'
She took a deep breath and he could tell that she was
struggling to control her emotions. 'Her husband is
almost beside himself with grief. She was six months

pregnant, you see, so he's lost both his wife and his unborn child.'

'Oh, hell!' He enfolded her in his arms, uncaring what anyone thought because he desperately wanted to comfort her. 'It's just not fair, is it?'

'No. It isn't.' Her voice was thickened with tears and he held her even tighter for a moment before she pulled away. 'Sorry. This is neither the time nor the place to start getting all emotional.'

'There's nothing to apologise for,' he countered, hating to hear her being so hard on herself. He experienced a sudden rush of concern when he saw how pale she looked. It was obvious the woman's death had affected her deeply, although it was hardly surprising in the circumstances.

'Why don't you go back to the hotel, Joanna?' he suggested. 'You've done more than enough here and you look worn out.'

'I'm fine.' She glanced round and sighed. 'Anyway, there's far too many people here who need help for me to go swanning off.'

'In that case then you may as well take over from me.' He handed her the X-ray. 'I'd better get myself into Theatre.'

'I believe a lot of the conference delegates are working in various hospitals around the city,' she told him, holding the X-ray up to the light.

'I suppose that's something to be grateful for. At least there isn't a shortage of qualified staff.' He glanced round when the nurse came to tell him that he was needed.

'Looks like that's my call to duty,' he said, turning to Joanna again. 'I'm not sure how long I'll be so why don't I meet you back at the hotel? You'll probably finish before I do and there's no point you waiting around.'

'Fine. Let me know when you get back, won't you?'

'I will.' He desperately wanted to kiss her but there was such an air of reserve about her that he decided not to risk upsetting her. He hurried across the crowded waiting-room and paused briefly outside the doors leading to Theatre, but Joanna was busy with the patient and didn't see him.

Dylan went straight to the changing room to get ready. Fortunately, the surgeon he was assisting spoke excellent English so there was no language barrier to contend with. They worked steadily until the queue of patients had been whittled away. Dylan shrugged off the other surgeon's thanks as they left Theatre. He'd been happy to help although he had to admit he was glad that it was time to leave. It was almost seven in the evening which meant—incredibly—that he'd been at the hospital for over six hours. Now what he wanted most was to go back to the hotel and find Joanna so they could carry on with their weekend.

The hotel's foyer was crowded when he got back. It appeared that a lot of the conference delegates were checking out. Dylan frowned as he made his way up in the lift. Had they decided to cut short their stay because of the bombing?

Joanna opened the door as soon as he knocked and let him into her room. 'How did it go?'

'Fine. We operated on three people and all of them should make it, I'm pleased to say.' He glanced across the room and frowned when he spotted her suitcase lying on the bed. 'Are you packing already?'

'Yes. The conference has been called off because of what's happened.'

'I see. That explains why there were so many people checking out just now. But it doesn't mean that we have to leave, surely? We aren't rostered to work this weekend so we can stay until Monday as we'd originally planned.'

'You can stay if you want to, of course, but I think it would be best if I returned home.'

She went to the bed and carefully packed a blouse into the case. Dylan watched her in stunned silence, wondering what had made her suddenly decide to go back to London. Was she worried in case there was another bomb scare, perhaps?

'If you're worried about there being another incident I'm sure the French police will be on full alert after what's happened,' he said gently.

'It's not that.' She placed a silk scarf in the case then closed the lid. 'I just feel it would be better if I went home tonight.'

'Better in which way?'

Dylan's heart was hammering so hard that he could actually *hear* it beating. He took a deep breath but it was difficult to appear calm when faced by this unexpected turn of events. Joanna had been fine when they'd last spoken. Granted, she'd been upset about the young mother who had died, but he honestly couldn't see how that would have had any bearing on her decision to leave.

'In all kinds of ways. Staying on in Paris won't achieve anything, Dylan. It will just make it that more difficult for us to return to normal once we're back at work.' She lifted the case off the bed and carried it over to the door.

Dylan ran a hand through his hair as he tried to make sense of what she'd said. 'I'm sorry, but I really don't see how it will make it more difficult. It's going to pretty damned hard to go back to the way we were after last night, whether or not we stay an extra couple of days.'

'I disagree. I think it will be a lot easier for both of us if I leave tonight.' She glanced round when there was a knock on the door. 'That will be the porter for my case. I've managed to get a seat on the Eurostar. It's due into London at midnight.'

'And what am I supposed to do, Joanna? Or don't you really care one way or the other?'

His anger rose on the back of a wave of pain so intense that it felt as though his heart was being ripped apart. If she'd stood there and told him—point blank—that she didn't care a jot about him the message couldn't have been any more clear.

'Of course I care, Dylan. If I didn't care I wouldn't be going home!'

'I'm sorry. Maybe I'm being particularly dense but that doesn't add up. Why would you decide to go home if you cared about my feelings?'

'Because I don't want you to make the mistake of falling in love with me.' Colour rose to her cheeks but she met his eyes without flinching. 'I've told you that we don't have a future and I meant it. I have worked far too hard to get where I am to throw it all away. Love, marriage and children are not on my agenda, Dylan, but they're on yours. It wouldn't be fair to let you lose out on all of those because you hope that I'll change my mind.'

There was a second knock on the door and she picked up her coat. 'I'm sorry if I've hurt you but one day you'll agree that I've made the right decision.'

'And what if I don't? What then, Joanna?' he asked hoarsely, but she just shook her head.

She opened the door and showed the porter her case then followed him from the room. Dylan stood right where he was, unmoving. His limbs felt too shaky to support him but even the few steps it would need to take him to the bed so he could sit down were too much.

He could scarcely believe that Joanna had undergone such a massive change of heart when everything had been fine a few hours ago. Had she been scared by the fact that he hadn't managed to hide his feelings for her?

He had tried his best not to let her see how much he cared about her but it wasn't easy when he loved her so much. Now he had to find a way to convince her that she was making a mistake by cutting him out of her life. She needed him just as much as he needed her…

Didn't she?

Dylan took a deep breath but the truth had to be faced. Joanna might never care as much about him as she cared about her career.

CHAPTER TEN

'SCALPEL... Damn!'

Joanna breathed deeply as the instrument slid through her fingers and dropped onto the theatre floor. It wasn't like her to be so clumsy but it was the third time that morning that she had managed to drop something. She nodded her thanks when Lucy handed her a fresh scalpel but she could tell the staff were wondering what was wrong with her. What would they think if she confessed that her lack of concentration was the result of missing Dylan?

She forced her mind back to the task at hand, knowing that she couldn't afford to let it wander. The patient, a woman in her forties called Mary Gregory, had been admitted with volvulus—a condition whereby a loop of intestines became twisted. According to the patient's notes Mary had been suffering from severe colic for several days and Joanna was concerned in case the blood supply to the affected tissue had been cut off.

She cut through the layers of fat and muscle in the abdominal wall until she reached the colon and sighed when she saw that her suspicions had been correct. There'd obviously been no blood supply to the area for some time and gangrene had set in. She would need to remove the dead tissue which would mean cutting away quite a large section of the colon then joining the two ends together again. It would take several weeks for the colon to fuse together so in the meantime its contents would need to be discharged through an artificial opening which she would have to make in the abdominal wall.

As she set to work, Joanne couldn't help wishing that Mary Gregory had sought help sooner rather than later because then she might not have needed to undergo such drastic treatment. It was usually best to face up to a problem rather than hope it would resolve itself.

That thought was a shade too close for comfort so Joanna put it out of her mind while she worked. An hour later she sent Mary Gregory to Recovery and went to get changed. There was a meeting with Brian Maxwell scheduled for that afternoon, when she and Dylan were supposed to report back about what had happened at the conference. Brian had been on holiday since they'd come home but he had phoned her that morning and set up the meeting. She was dreading it.

For the past two weeks she had gone out of her way to avoid Dylan but there was no way that she could avoid him that day. The thought of being in the same room as him made her feel sick with guilt. Even though she was sure that she'd been right to call a halt when she had, it didn't make the situation any easier. She only had to remember the look on his face when she'd told him she was going home to know how much she'd hurt him, yet what else could she have done?

Witnessing that young Frenchman's grief at losing his wife and unborn child had made her see how wrong it would be to encourage Dylan's growing feelings for her. Granted, their situation might be rather different but there could be no justification for knowingly breaking someone's heart. She couldn't and *wouldn't* allow Dylan to fall in love with her when she had nothing to offer him in return.

Joanna showered and dressed then went to her office to check if there were any messages for her. Lisa was at lunch but she'd left a list of calls on her desk. Joanna glanced through them but as there was nothing urgent she decided to deal with them later. She needed to clear her head before the meeting and a walk round the park might help. She was just leaving her office when Diane Grant, the surgical consultant, hailed her.

'Have you got a minute, Joanna? I need a word with you.'

'Of course. Come in.' Joanna unlocked the door and went back inside. She waved Diane towards a chair and sat down. 'I was just going to take a breather before my meeting with Brian Maxwell.'

'I didn't realise you had a meeting,' Diane said hurriedly. 'Shall I leave it till later?'

'No, it's fine. Don't worry. To be honest, I don't know why I'm bothering to go. Brian wants to know what went on at the conference, but there isn't that much to tell him seeing as it was called off.'

'I heard about that. Bad luck.' Diane grinned. She was an attractive woman in her late thirties with short, red hair and an engaging smile. 'The one time you manage to get a free trip to Paris and something like that has to happen!'

'Typical, isn't it?' Joanna agreed lightly, not wanting to be drawn into a discussion about what had happened during that weekend. Her heart jolted when the memory of waking in Dylan's arms on the Saturday morning flashed into her mind. She couldn't remember ever having felt so cherished before. Oh, she'd had lovers in the past but none had made her feel so special. The thought brought a rush of tears to her eyes and she hurriedly blinked them away.

'It is,' Diane agreed. 'Anyway, I won't keep you, seeing as you were on your way out. I just thought I'd give you advance warning that I'm leaving.'

'Really?' Joanna looked at the other woman in surprise. 'I didn't know you were looking for another job, Diane.'

'I'm not. The reason I've decided to leave is because I want to spend more time with Matthew.' Diane grimaced. 'I was so sure that I'd be able to combine being a mum with doing my job but it's not as easy as I thought it would be. I miss being with him so much that it's a real wrench having to leave him each morning so I've decided to hand in my notice.'

'Are you sure you won't regret it? You know that once you step off the professional ladder it's going to be very difficult to get back on it again,' Joanna warned.

'I understand that but my priorities have changed since I had the baby. Matthew comes first now and Gerry and I both agree that it's the right thing to do.' Diane laughed. 'I can tell you think I'm mad but I want to be a real mum to him far more than I ever wanted to be a top-notch surgeon, amazingly enough!'

'Then all I can say is that I hope it works out for you, Diane. I appreciate you letting me know, although it's not going to be easy to replace you.'

'Oh, I don't know about that. Dylan Archer is shaping up rather well from what I've seen. He's due for a consultancy soon and I think he could step into my shoes with very little problem.'

'We'll see.' Joanna summoned a smile as she opened her diary. Diane was right because Dylan would make an ideal replacement. In other circumstances she would have been relieved to know that she had someone so capable already on her team, but all she could think about was how difficult it was going to be, working with him on a long-term basis when the past two weeks had been such a strain.

'So when were you thinking of handing in your notice?' she asked, trying not to dwell on the problems she'd created for herself.

'Today, actually. I was only waiting until I'd spoken to you before I set everything in motion,' Diane admitted.

'And today is—what? The twenty-third of April?' Joanna flicked through the pages of the diary, frowning when she came to the one she wanted. She'd lost track of the time and hadn't realised how fast the month was rushing past. She looked up when Diane explained that she was planning to leave at the end of May, after she had worked out her notice, but even though Joanna responded, she couldn't shake off the feeling that there was something she'd overlooked.

Fortunately, Diane didn't prolong the meeting. She stood up and smiled at Joanna. 'I hope you don't think that I'm leaving you in the lurch, Joanna, but I feel as though I'm being torn in two at the moment. You're really lucky because you're so single-minded. Your work is everything to you, isn't it?'

'Yes,' she agreed rather flatly, not sure she enjoyed having that pointed out to her. 'Work has always come first with me.'

She got up after Diane left and went into the tiny bathroom adjoining her office. It was too late to go for a walk now so she may as well get ready for the meeting. She washed her hands and tidied her hair, sighing as she studied her reflection. Diane was right because she'd always known what she had wanted out of life from the time she'd been a teenager, but had it been a mistake to set her sights on a career at the expense of a personal life? Her career might have given her a sense of self-worth which she'd been lacking while she'd been growing up, but it hadn't eased the ache in her heart which had been with her constantly since she'd come back from Paris two weeks ago.

Joanna's breath caught when the significance of those words struck her. It was two weeks since she'd come home and in that time she'd not had her normal monthly period! That was what had been bothering her while she'd been talking to Diane—being reminded about the date had set the alarm bells ringing.

She ran back into office and flicked back through the pages of her diary, feeling her heart sink when she saw that her period was three days overdue. Her menstrual cycle had always been extremely regular and she had never been even a day late before.

She sank down onto a chair as her legs suddenly gave way. She and Dylan hadn't used any kind of protection when they'd made love—they hadn't even thought about it. They had been so carried away by their feelings that they had given no thought to the consequences of what they'd been doing. Of course, it could be that the emotional turmoil she'd suffered recently had affected her cycle, but there was a very strong chance that she was pregnant. She had no idea what she was going to do if it turned out to be true but she would worry about that after she'd found out for certain.

Joanna left her office and hurried to the lift. There was a chemist's shop not far from the hospital so she went there and bought three different pregnancy testing kits. She went straight into the bathroom when she got back to her office and read the instructions on the packages, thinking how ironic it was that she, a doctor, should find herself in this predicament. She still had no idea what she was going to do if she was pregnant, but one thing was certain. She wasn't going to tell Dylan. She didn't want him thinking that he had to stand by her for the sake of the child!

'It's a pity the conference had to be cut short. I'm sure Joanna would agree that we learned a great deal even in the short time we were there.'

Dylan tried to sound positive but he could tell that Brian Maxwell was becoming increasingly impatient. He checked his watch when Brian excused himself to take a phone call, wondering where Joanna had got to. The meeting had been scheduled for two o'clock and it was half past the hour now yet there was still no sign of her. Surely she hadn't decided not to attend because she'd wanted to avoid him?

The thought was too painful to contemplate so he focused instead on giving Brian a full report on what had gone on during the weekend. He'd stayed on in Paris until the Monday morning, spending the rest of his time there helping out at Sancerre Hospital. He had considered flying home on the Sunday morning, but the thought of sitting in his flat, going over and over what had happened, had been more than he could bear. He'd decided it would be better to keep busy and worry about changing Joanna's mind at a later date.

He sighed because that seemed like wishful thinking now. Joanna had said barely a word to him in the past two weeks so the likelihood of him being able to convince her that she'd been wrong to cut him out of her life seemed very remote. Still, faint heart never won fair lady, according to the old adage, so he wasn't going to give up just yet.

The meeting finally came to an end and Dylan left the director's office. He would have liked to have checked on Joanna and find out what had happened to her, but he had a ward round to do first. He went straight to the surgical ward and gathered up the rest of the crew who were waiting for him. They had a couple of students with them that week, plus a brand new houseman, so there was quite a crowd when they set off.

Thankfully, there were no real problems, although Sarah Rothwell seemed extremely anxious about a patient they would be operating on the following day. Dylan borrowed the ward sister's office while he talked Sarah through the procedure until he was sure that she was happy about what she would have to do. She tended to worry far too much about making a mistake and he made a note to speak to Joanna about her. It could turn out that Sarah wasn't suited for surgery and it would be better if she accepted that rather than spend her life in a state of perpetual anxiety. You had to want to do this job more than anything else in the world if you hoped to survive the pressures that came with it.

That thought, naturally, reminded him about Joanna's dedication. Dylan frowned as he left the ward. Was he being selfish to expect her to take risks with the career she had worked so hard for? He knew how difficult it was for a woman to succeed in surgery because he'd witnessed at first hand the chauvinistic attitude of many of his fellow surgeons. That Joanna had reached such a high level was a wonderful achievement. Maybe he should reassure her that he understood how important her job was to her and make sure she knew that he would never expect her to give it up? There *must* be a way to make their relationship work.

Dylan's heart lifted with a sudden resurgence of optimism. He went straight to Joanna's office, not wanting to waste another minute. Lisa was at her desk and she shook her head when he opened the door. 'If you're looking for Ms Archer, she's not here, I'm afraid.'

'Oh. Right. D'you know where she's gone?' Dylan asked, trying not to feel deflated by the setback.

'I've no idea but the phone's been ringing non-stop all afternoon with people wanting to speak to her.' Lisa sighed. 'She disappeared as soon as I got back from lunch and I've not heard a word from her since.'

'And she didn't say where she was going?' Dylan confirmed, because it was so unlike Joanna to go missing.

'No. I asked her where she'd be if anyone wanted her but I don't think she heard me. She seemed to be acting rather…well, oddly.'

'What do you mean? Was she ill?' he demanded in concern.

'No-o…not ill exactly. Distracted is the best way to describe her mood. It was as though she was in a bit of daze.' Lisa shrugged. 'She probably has a lot on her mind, I imagine.'

'I expect so. Thanks, Lisa.'

Dylan summoned a smile but he couldn't deny that he was worried. He left the office and decided to check if Joanna was in Theatre. Maybe an emergency had cropped up which would explain why she had failed to turn up for the meeting. However, the theatre staff hadn't seen her since that morning. He checked the wards next in case she had gone to visit a patient but once again drew a blank. He finally phoned the switchboard and asked them to page her, but it appeared her pager was switched off.

Dylan thanked the operator and hung up. Something must have happened because it was unheard of for Joanna to turn off her pager. Although he suspected that she wouldn't welcome his interference, he wouldn't rest until he made sure she was all right. He had her address from when he'd taken her home after the Royal College of Surgeons dinner so he would go round to her flat.

Determination lit his eyes as he hurried upstairs for his coat. Of course, Joanna might refuse to see him but he didn't intend to take no for an answer. He was going to get to the bottom of what was going on.

Joanna paced the sitting-room floor, wondering what to do. The pregnancy tests had all proved positive so there was no doubt now that she was having Dylan's baby. She couldn't believe how stupid she'd been to get herself in this situation but there was no point dwelling on that now. She had two choices—she could have the baby or she could have a termination.

The doorbell suddenly chimed and she swung round, wondering who could be visiting her at that time of the day. She went to the entry phone and pressed the button to speak to the caller. 'Yes?'

'It's me, Joanna. Will you let me in, please?'

Joanna's heart leapt into her throat when she recognised Dylan's voice. He was the last person she wanted to see at the present moment. 'I'm sorry but it isn't convenient right now.'

'Then I'll just have to wait here until it is convenient.'

The line went dead and she slowly replaced the receiver, wondering what he'd meant by that. Surely he didn't intend to wait outside until she decided to let him in?

She ran to the window and gasped when she saw Dylan sitting down on a bench opposite the entrance to the apartment block. It was pouring with rain but he seemed oblivious to the weather as he settled himself on the bench as though he was prepared to stay there all night if need be. Joanna's mouth pursed. If he was foolish enough to sit there getting soaked that was his decision, but she refused to give in to emotional blackmail!

She managed to hold out for almost an hour until the sound of the rain drumming against the window panes finally made her cave in. She pressed the button to unlock the main doors then waited for him to come upstairs. He was soaking wet when she let him into the flat and she glared at him as he dripped water all over her floor.

'You must be mad to sit outside in all that rain!'

'Probably. Still, it worked, didn't it?' He grinned as he eased himself out of his sodden overcoat. 'I knew you wouldn't leave me there to catch my death.'

Joanna didn't say anything as she took the coat off him and carried it into the bathroom so it could drip into the bath. Dylan followed her so she tossed him a towel off the rail. 'Here.'

'Thanks.' He quickly towelled his hair then finger-combed it into place and smiled at her. Joanna felt her heart squeeze out an extra couple of beats when she saw the warmth in his eyes. 'I feel almost human again. There's nothing better than coming inside out of the elements.'

'Don't get too comfortable,' she warned, knowing it would be a mistake to weaken. If Dylan found out about the baby he would do his utmost to make her keep it. She had to base her decision on common sense, not emotion, and do what was right for everyone.

It was a sobering thought and she couldn't deny how nervous she felt as she led the way into the sitting room. 'You have five minutes to tell me what you want and then I expect you to leave.'

'Now, now, Joanna, that isn't very hospitable. Especially not when I've come here to see if you're all right.'

'I'm fine. Why shouldn't I be?' she snapped, her heart lurching in alarm. Surely Dylan didn't suspect what was wrong with her?

'Because first of all you missed the meeting with Brian Maxwell and then you went home without telling anyone.' He sat down and studied her quietly. 'You also switched off your pager and it's just not like you, Joanna. Something has happened and I want to know what's wrong.'

'There's nothing wrong! I just decided to go home early for once.'

'I see. So you don't feel ill?'

'No, I'm fine.' She stood up and looked pointedly at the door but Dylan ignored her. Short of physically ejecting him, she couldn't think how to make him leave so she sat down again.

'Now we've established that you're feeling OK

maybe we could sort out a few other issues?' His voice had deepened and she wrapped her arms around herself to ward off the shivers that were suddenly racing through her. He'd used that same tone in Paris and it was hard not to think about those wonderful hours they'd spent making love.

'We said all that needed to be said a couple of weeks ago,' she replied brusquely, struggling to rid herself of the memories.

'No, we didn't,' he corrected gently. 'You told me how you felt, Joanna, but you didn't give me a chance to explain how I feel.' He held up his hand when she went to speak. 'No, please, hear me out. You told me that you didn't want me to fall in love with you but I'm afraid it's too late. I fell in love with you almost as soon as we met and there's not much I can do about it, I'm afraid.'

His smile was so full of tenderness that her eyes prickled with tears. 'Please don't,' she implored, standing up. 'I don't want to hear this, Dylan.'

'I'm sure you don't, but I want to tell you.' He stood up as well, putting out a restraining hand when she tried to move away. 'I love you, Joanna, and I think that we could have something really special if you would give us a chance. I know you're worried about the effect it could have on your career if we had a relationship, but I really and truly believe that we could make it work.'

He cupped her face between his hands and his eyes were as dark as the ocean on a stormy night when he looked at her. 'I know how important your work is to you and I promise that I shall always respect that. You were right when you said that I've always wanted a family, but I can live without having children if it isn't what you want. I need *you*, Joanna, and I'm sure that if you'll only find the courage to look into your heart you'll see that you need me, too.'

'No, you're wrong.' Joanna could feel tears welling in her eyes but she couldn't allow herself to cry. Dylan's words had touched her deeply but she had to think with her head, not her heart. Maybe he truly believed that he could forgo having a family for the sake of her career, but she wasn't convinced. If he found out that she was pregnant would he support her if she decided not to have the baby? And if she did have it how could she be sure that Dylan wasn't staying with her for the child's sake?

She mustn't forget that she was older than him and the age gap could cause problems in the future. Although he might love her now, there was no guarantee that his feelings would last. Her parents had never really wanted her so she had grown up feeling like an encumbrance; she had got in the way and they had resented that. She couldn't bear to think that she might find herself in the same position again, couldn't cope with the thought that at some point Dylan might wish that he had never met her.

It would break her heart, she realised with a sudden flash of insight, and that was why she had to put a stop to this now. She would risk breaking Dylan's heart and her own if she let it continue.

'I don't need you, Dylan. I'm sorry but there's no other way to say this. I don't love you and I can't imagine that I ever will.'

An expression of anguish crossed his face as he let her go. Joanna held herself rigid because the urge to put her arms around him and beg his forgiveness was almost too strong to resist, but she mustn't weaken.

She was doing this for his sake, first and foremost, but it was hard to remember that when she could see how much she had hurt him.

'Then all I can do is apologise if I've embarrassed you, Joanna. It was the last thing I intended to do.'

'You haven't embarrassed me,' she denied, not wanting to add to his distress.

'You're very kind.' He glanced towards the door. 'May I have my coat, please? I think I should leave.'

'Yes, of course.' She hurried from the room, wondering if she would ever feel this wretched again. Dylan was doing his best to hide his feelings but she knew how much he was hurting.

Tears ran down her cheeks as she unhooked his coat from the shower rail. It was still soaking wet but she held it against her face while she drank in the faint scent of his aftershave that clung to the damp wool. It was so poignant to stand there surrounded by Dylan's scent, to hold his coat in her arms and know that his child was growing inside her, that a sob escaped her then another until all of a sudden she was crying in earnest. It was all such a mess, such a horrible mess!

'Don't! Please, don't cry, my darling. I can't bear it.'

Suddenly Dylan was there, gathering her and the sodden coat into his arms and holding them both tightly against him. Joanna laid her head on his chest as the tears streamed down her face.

'I never meant to hurt you,' she whispered brokenly.

'I know. I never meant to upset you like this either.' His hands were warm and gentle on her cheeks as he dried her tears, almost as gentle as his lips when he bent and kissed her with a tenderness that made her soul ache. He drew back and it was a measure of the man he was that he managed to smile at her despite what she'd done. 'Friends, Joanna?'

'Friends,' she repeated, wondering if they could ever be friends after what had happened.

She saw him out then went back to the sitting room and sat there, staring at the familiar trappings of her life. This was her home, the place she returned to after her working day ended, but it looked so empty now that Dylan had left, so sterile and barren and lacking in meaning.

She closed her eyes and tried to picture another kind of life than the one she had created for herself and felt her heart ache afresh when the image of a small boy with black curls and sea-green eyes took shape.

She opened her eyes abruptly but the picture didn't fade. It stayed with her for the rest of the night, an image of Dylan's child, the child she was carrying beneath her heart. How could she bear to part with it when she loved its father so much?

CHAPTER ELEVEN

THE days seemed to drag so that Dylan started to feel as though he was trapped in a never-ending cycle of working and going home to an empty flat. He still found it difficult to accept Joanna's decision and lay awake at night thinking about what she'd said. Even though she'd told him that she could never love him, he kept trying to think of ways to change her mind. Although she had stopped avoiding him, their conversations were always confined to work and never once touched upon anything personal. It didn't stop him noticing how strained she looked, though, and it puzzled him. For a woman who claimed to be so sure about her feelings, she seemed to have a lot on her mind. He resolved to find out what was wrong but it was almost a month after he'd been to visit her at home that he had an inkling about what was wrong.

He'd just left Theatre one afternoon after a particularly stressful session. The patient had a history of cardiac trouble and Dylan had needed to work fast to minimise the risks. He had asked specifically for Tom to act as his anaesthetist because of the problems involved in sedating the man. There had been a couple of hairy moments but, all things considered, the operation had gone far better than he'd dared hope.

He smiled his thanks as Tom followed him into the changing room.

'That was a first-rate job, Tom, not that I need to tell you that, of course.'

'It never hurts to receive the odd compliment,' Tom returned airily. 'You didn't do too bad yourself, although a couple of those staples looked a bit wonky from my end of the table.'

'I'll remember to bring my spirit level into Theatre next time,' he retorted, wadding his dirty scrub suit into a ball and tossing it into the laundry hamper.

'Good idea. Still, at least you didn't go rushing off midway through the operation. That's something to be thankful for.' Tom's voice was muffled as he dragged his scrub suit top over his head.

'I should hope so.' Dylan frowned. 'Who exactly are we talking about here? Don't tell me young Sarah had another crisis of confidence?'

'No, although I can't see her lasting much longer. The poor kid's a bundle of nerves.' Tom took a towel off the shelf. 'It was Joanna, actually. We'd barely got started this morning when she suddenly went dashing off. Lucy told me that it's the third time it's happened this week and that when she went after her yesterday, she found her throwing up.'

'I thought she'd been looking rather pale recently. Maybe she's caught some sort of tummy bug,' Dylan suggested, trying not to sound too concerned.

'Maybe. And maybe not.' Tom winked. 'Far be it from me to start speculating about such matters but it doesn't take a genius to add up the clues. Looking peaky and throwing up each morning could be a sign of something more than a tummy bug.'

'You think she might be pregnant?' Dylan exclaimed in shock.

'I know. It sounds unlikely, doesn't it? Joanna has always seemed more concerned about her career than anything else. I'd never have thought she would con-

sider having a child, although maybe she didn't plan
on it happening. Accidents can and do happen as we
all know to our cost.'

Tom wandered off to the showers but Dylan stayed
where he was. He felt as though he'd been rooted to
the spot with shock. Was it possible that Joanna was
pregnant? And if she was then who was the baby's
father?

His mind raced back to their trip to Paris and his
heart began to pound. He had never even thought
about using any contraception! The moment he'd
taken Joanna in his arms every sensible thought had
fled. Now the idea that Joanna might be having his
child made him feel so mixed up that it was hard to
think what to do. Should be ask her point blank if she
was pregnant or should he wait for her to tell him?

His head was reeling as he went into the shower.
He dried himself off afterwards, barely hearing a word
Tom said. Fortunately, Tom had patients to see so he
ambled off, giving Dylan a much-needed breathing
space.

He quickly dressed then made his way downstairs.
There was an outpatients clinic that day and he had a
list of patients to see so he couldn't go rushing off to
speak to Joanna just yet. He would have to wait until
later to find out if she was having his baby.

A rush of elation filled him at the thought of what
it could mean. Joanna wouldn't be able to shut him
out of her life if she was having his child! Maybe it
wasn't the way he had planned things to happen but
he loved her too much to pass up the opportunity. The
thought that he might be a part of her life in the future
filled him with joy. He couldn't imagine anything bet-

ter than having Joanna and his child to love and cherish, to care for in the years ahead...

If there was a child, the voice of reason cautioned. And he had no proof yet that there was.

Dylan took a deep breath. He didn't know how he was going to cope until he found out the truth.

'Everything looks fine, Mrs Gregory. The scar has healed nicely, which is always a good sign.' Joanna smiled reassuringly at the two women. Mary Gregory had brought her daughter with her to the outpatients clinic and it was obvious the young woman was extremely concerned about her mother.

'But how soon can Mum get rid of that awful bag thing, Ms Martin?' Alison Gregory demanded. 'I don't mean to sound unkind but it makes me feel really sick when I think of her having that attached to her for ever!'

'Once I'm sure the two sections of colon have fused together I shall reverse the colostomy,' Joanna explained gently. Many patients and their relatives had difficulty accepting the need for a colostomy. 'I shall then close the opening in the abdominal wall and all your mother will be left with will be a small scar.'

'See, I told you, didn't I, Alison? The nurse who taught me how to change the bag explained that it was only temporary.' Mary Gregory turned to Joanna and smiled. 'I expect it's different when you're Alison's age but it really doesn't worry me. I'm just so grateful for what you did. The nurse told me that I could have died if you hadn't operated.'

'Thankfully, everything has turned out very well,' Joanna replied lightly. 'Anyway, I shall schedule you for surgery to reverse the colostomy in a few weeks' time. You'll receive an appointment through the post. In the meantime, just carry on the way you've been doing and you shouldn't have any problems.'

Joanna sank back in her chair after Mary and Alison Gregory left. They'd been her last patients, thankfully. She'd found herself getting increasingly tired in the past week, although whether that was due to her pregnancy or other factors was difficult to decide. She could understand that physical symptoms like the awful morning sickness that she'd been suffering of late were all part and parcel of being pregnant. However, the depression that seemed to hang over her like a dark cloud each day was probably more emotional than anything else.

She still hadn't decided what she was going to do—whether she was going to keep the baby or have a termination—and the uncertainty was tearing her apart. In her heart she knew that she wanted this child but the rational part of her knew it would be wrong to have it. It wasn't just her life that would be changed for ever by the birth of this child, but Dylan's as well. Was she really prepared to put him through any more than he'd suffered already?

She got up, unable to sit there while her mind raced with all those questions. Gathering together the files, she started towards the door then paused when someone knocked. Sighing, she put the folders back on the desk. 'Come in.'

'I was hoping I'd catch you.'

Joanna's heart lurched when Dylan came into the room. Just for a second her eyes drank in every detail, from the shadows under his beautiful green eyes to the lines of strain that bracketed his mouth. Every time they had spoken in the past few weeks she'd had to physically restrain herself from touching him, and it was the same again that day. When he came over to her she wanted to take hold of his hand and feel his fingers curling so warmly and comfortingly around hers, but she didn't dare give in to the urge. She could look but not touch, otherwise she wouldn't be able to stop herself telling him about the baby and it would be wrong to do that, very wrong indeed to make him think that she expected him to take care of her and the child. The baby had been an accident and she knew only too well the problems an unwanted child could cause.

'I was just on my way upstairs,' she explained, her heart aching as the memories of her lonely childhood came rushing back. If she had this child she would make sure he knew just how much he was loved. She would never do to her child what her own parents had done to her and treat it with indifference!

'I won't keep you, then. I just wanted to clear something up.' He came closer, staring at her in a way that made her feel incredibly nervous. 'When we slept together in Paris we didn't use any form of contraception. I'll be perfectly honest and admit that I never even thought about it or about the possible consequences of not using it.'

He took her hands and held them just as she'd imagined him doing, only now she could feel the tension oozing from him as his fingers gripped hers. 'I want you to tell me the truth, Joanna. Are you pregnant?'

Dylan could feel his heart thumping. Joanna was staring at him and the horror on her face would have been amusing if there'd been anything remotely funny about the situation. When she snatched her hands away he didn't try to stop her, couldn't have done while he was having so much difficulty maintaining his self-control.

'I've no idea what makes you imagine I'm pregnant,' she began haughtily.

'Tom told me about you rushing out of Theatre this morning to be sick,' he said flatly. 'Evidently, it's the third time it's happened this week.'

'And that's your proof, is it?' She laughed scornfully but he could tell how shaken she was and knew that Tom was right. Joanna *was* pregnant, even though she was going to deny it for as long as she could.

'That and the fact that we made love six weeks ago without taking any precautions against having a baby.' He shrugged when she fell silent. 'Obviously, I have no proof that I'm able to father a child, but as I have nothing to prove that I can't let's simply assume that I am capable of reproducing. I don't know of any reason why you can't have children, although admittedly I don't know much about your medical history.

'Add all that to the rest of the facts and it seems perfectly feasible that we could have created a baby. I mean, we made love—several times, actually—and the basic facts of human reproduction state that if at least one of my sperm managed to find its way to your egg then the result should be seven or eight pounds of bouncing baby once the necessary nine months have elapsed. Do you agree with me so far?'

'I...um...'

'Good.' Dylan summoned a smile, relieved he wasn't causing her too much distress. He didn't want to upset her but this issue needed to be resolved.

His racing heart somehow managed to race even faster as he briefly allowed himself to imagine the baby which might be growing inside Joanna's womb, but he really shouldn't dwell on such thoughts at this stage. He had to get her to tell him the truth before he got carried away.

'So now we've established all that, let me ask you the question again, Joanna. Are you pregnant?'

An expression of indecision crossed her face before she pulled her hands away and stalked to the window. 'Yes. And before you ask, *yes*, the baby is yours, Dylan.'

Dylan felt a wave of intense relief wash over him and sank down onto the edge of the desk. 'Thank you,' he said quietly.

'What for?'

'For being honest with me. I know how hard it must have been for you, Joanna.'

She shrugged, keeping her face averted as she stared out of the window. 'These things have to be faced up to, the same as I need to face up to what I'm going to do about it.'

'What do you mean?' he said slowly, wondering why he had a sudden feeling that he wasn't going to like this.

'That I haven't decided yet if I'm keeping the child.'

'You're considering having a termination?' he demanded, unable to keep the shock out of his voice.

'It's an option.'

'Not from where I'm standing it isn't!' he snapped, jumping to his feet.

'It isn't your decision, Dylan. It's mine.'

'Maybe it is your decision but I should have a say in it, surely? Damn it, Joanna, this is my child we're discussing. It isn't just up to you to decide whether it should live or die!'

'I'm afraid in the eyes of the law you have absolutely no say in the matter.' Her tone was icily cold but he could see the pain in her eyes and it was that more than anything which helped him calm down. Finding out that she was pregnant must have been a shock for her and he should be doing all he could to reassure her rather than laying down the law.

'I know and I apologise for jumping down your throat like that.' He shrugged. 'It's hard to be dispassionate when you're personally involved.'

'Which is why it would have been so much better if you'd never found out.'

He winced. 'So you weren't going to tell me? You were going to have a termination and I'd have been none the wiser.'

'I haven't made up my mind what I'm going to do yet. I wasn't going to tell you because I knew how you would react and I wanted to base my decision on common sense rather than…emotion.'

'We're talking about a baby here so I don't think it's possible to be unemotional.' He got up and went to the window but he didn't touch her. He couldn't trust himself to do that because he knew he would fall apart. He wanted her to have this child so much that it was like a physical ache, but it would be wrong to force her to do something she might regret. He had to try and persuade her they could work this out but it wasn't going to be easy, especially not when he remembered his previous attempts to change her mind and how they had ended.

'I know this must have been a shock for you, Joanna, and I understand why you're worried about the problems it could cause. However, I want you to know that I will do everything I can to help if you decide to keep the baby.'

'Thank you. I appreciate that.'

Her tone was so distant that his heart froze over because he sensed he wasn't getting through to her. 'I didn't offer out of politeness or out of a sense of duty.'

He turned to face her, willing her to look at him, but she kept staring out of the window. 'I've never made any secret of how I feel about you and this child will be even more special because of that. I love you, Joanna, and I can think of nothing I want more than to spend my life with you and our baby. If you're worried about your career then we'll find a way to get around any problems. I could give up work to look after the child, if that's what you want.'

'You'd do that?' she said, glancing at him, and he saw the surprise in her beautiful grey eyes.

'Yes. My career means a lot to me but you mean more. It's your happiness that is the most important thing of all.'

'But if I did have the baby—and I've not made up my mind yet—then who's to say that your feelings won't change? I'm seven years older than you, Dylan, and you could meet someone younger in a few years time, a woman who could give you more children— that family you've always dreamed of having.'

'It won't happen.' He spun her round, too impatient to convince her that he meant what he said to waste any more time. 'It's you I love. You and only you! My feelings won't change this year, next year or ten years down the line from now. Understand?'

'Yes.'

Tears brimmed from her eyes and Dylan gathered

her into his arms and hugged her. 'Sh, sweetheart, there's no need to cry. There's nothing to be scared of. I won't let anything hurt you or our baby.'

He tried to draw her closer but she pushed him away. His heart seemed to stall when he saw the shuttered expression on her face because it was the last thing he'd hoped to see. He didn't want her shutting him out like this when he needed to convince her he was telling the truth.

'I know you believe what you're saying but nobody can keep a promise like that, Dylan. You just don't know how you'll feel in a few years' time. You could come to resent me and this child and I couldn't bear that.'

'So what exactly are you saying?' he asked hoarsely.

'That I don't know what I'm going to do but I do know that any decision I make has to be mine.' She drew herself up and there was a dignity about her that almost broke his heart.

'And it makes no difference what I say?'

'No.' Her eyes swam with tears again but she didn't flinch. 'I have to know in my own heart that I'm doing the right thing. If I allow you to persuade me we could both regret it.'

'I think you're wrong to try and solve this problem all by yourself, Joanna. I *know* you're wrong.' Frustration laced his voice and turned it harsh but he couldn't help that. 'I love you and my feelings won't change even when we're old and grey. Just because your parents made you feel unwanted it doesn't mean that I will ever stop wanting you.'

He touched her mouth with his fingertips, felt it tremble and let his hand fall to his side because it was too painful to witness her distress. 'I love you, my darling. And I shall love our child as well if you decide to have it.'

He quickly left the office because he couldn't bear to stay there a moment longer. She'd said that she hadn't made up her mind about what she was going to do, but he was terrified that, deep down, she already knew what the outcome was going to be.

Tears clouded his vision as he made his way to the lift. The thought that Joanna might decide not to keep their child was so painful yet it was the fact that she was still intent on shutting him out of her life that hurt even more. In that moment he knew that he couldn't stay at St Leonard's because it would be far too difficult for them to work together from now on. He would leave and find another job, try to put his life back together again, only it wasn't going to be easy when his heart wouldn't be in it.

His heart would remain here with Joanna…for ever.

'I was really surprised when Dylan told me he was leaving at the end of the month. It was rather a bolt from the blue, wasn't it?'

'I suppose so.'

Joanna elbowed the taps shut then took the towel Lucy offered her with a murmur of thanks. Dylan had left a note on her desk, tersely informing her than he had handed in his notice that morning, and she was still reeling from the shock of discovering that he'd be leaving. It was an effort to concentrate when Lucy continued the conversation.

'I wonder why he's decided to leave so suddenly. D'you think it could be woman trouble?'

'I've no idea,' she replied shortly, hoping Lucy would let the matter drop.

'It seems the most likely explanation, doesn't it, although I've not heard any rumours about him being involved with anyone from the hospital.' Lucy moved behind her to fasten the ties on her Theatre gown. 'Dylan's such a babe that most of the nurses here would give their right arms to go out with him but, to my knowledge, he's never asked anyone out since he started working here.'

'Really.' Joanna heard the bite in her voice and knew that Lucy must have heard it, too. She summoned a smile, not wanting to arouse the other woman's suspicions. 'Sorry, I didn't mean to sound so grouchy.'

'That's OK. I expect it's a bit of bind, having to think about finding someone to replace him, especially when you must have a lot of other things on your mind...'

Lucy broke off as she realised that she might have said too much. Joanna sighed as she headed into Theatre. Everyone was speculating about whether or not she was pregnant and it just seemed to increase the pressure on her to reach a decision about what she was going to do. She couldn't keep putting it off much longer or she wouldn't have a choice at all.

Sadness filled her because she knew that she'd been procrastinating because she didn't want to have to make the decision. She wanted this baby so much but would it be right to have it in the circumstances? Would it be fair to Dylan to bind him to her with a child they hadn't planned?

Once again it was impossible to answer those questions so Joanna took refuge in her work. Thankfully, the ginger tea and arrowroot biscuits she'd eaten when she'd got up had managed to stave off the dreaded morning sickness so she didn't need to go rushing out of Theatre. She worked her way through her morning list and broke for lunch then went back for the afternoon session. Dylan was taking the referrals clinic that day and it was a relief to know that she wouldn't bump into him. She'd almost finished her final operation for the day—a prostatectomy on a middle-aged man who had a very enlarged prostate gland—when there was a commotion outside in the corridor.

'What on earth is going on out there?' she demanded, glancing up.

'I've no idea,' Lucy replied as the sound of raised voices issued along the corridor.

'Go and see what's happening, will you? I've just about finished in here.'

Joanna tied off the last stitch then checked that the drainage tube which would remove blood and fluid from the area was secure. She looked round when Lucy came rushing back into Theatre. 'What's happened?'

'Apparently some chap just pulled out a gun in A and E. The security staff tried to grab him and it went off.'

'Good heavens!' Joanna exclaimed. 'Was anyone hurt?'

'Yes.' Lucy swallowed and Joanna could see tears welling into her eyes. 'Dylan had been asked to check on a patient so he was in A and E when it happened. H-he's been shot in the chest and it doesn't look good. Diane's taken him straight to Theatre but no one knows if he's going to survive.'

CHAPTER TWELVE

DYLAN had been in Theatre for almost three hours and there was still no news.

Joanna paced the corridor, wondering what she was going to do if he died. She loved him so much that she would have happily traded places with him if it had been possible. All she could do was to pray that he would make it because if he did she wasn't going to waste another second of the time they had left to them. She was going to tell him that she loved him and beg him to forgive her...

'Joanna.'

She swung round when she recognised Diane's voice. 'How is he?' she demanded hoarsely.

'He's alive, so that's something. The bullet just missed his heart. It passed above the left atrium and went straight into his left shoulder. It ended up in the glenoid cavity.'

'What about tissue damage?'

'Quite extensive, as is usually the case with a high-velocity gunshot wound. It's hard to say exactly how much damage has been done at this stage but there could be a problem regaining full mobility of the arm because of the injury to the socket. I had to remove several fragments of bone.'

Diane glanced along the corridor to where the rest of the staff were gathered. Nobody had gone home after their shift had ended because they'd been too worried about Dylan. Joanna nodded towards them.

'Go and tell the others that he's all right. We can talk again later. Is it OK if I go in and see him?'

'Of course. He'll be transferred to ICU pretty soon. Fortunately, they had a bed free for once. I'll catch up with you later.'

Joanna went into Recovery while Diane went to speak to the rest of the staff. There was a nurse there and she smiled at Joanna.

'Hi, Ms Martin. He's hanging in, I'm pleased to say. Want to take a look?'

'Please.' Joanna stepped forward as the nurse moved aside. She felt a lump come to a throat when she saw Dylan lying on the bed. There were tubes supplying him with oxygen and other vital fluids. His left shoulder had been heavily padded with gauze but she could see blood seeping through the dressing. He was attached to a monitor and one glance was sufficient to tell her that his pulse was still very erratic. Shock was always a huge factor in this type of injury, plus blood loss and nerve damage and...

She didn't realise she was crying until the nurse handed her a tissue. She dried her eyes, uncaring if she was making a fool of herself. She loved this man more than anything in the world and it scared her to see him lying there and know that he might die. When the porters arrived to take him to the IC unit, Joanna went with them, holding Dylan's hand as they wheeled the trolley to the lift. Even though he was heavily sedated, it was possible that he could sense she was there and she clung to that thought.

The staff on the IC unit were expecting them but Joanna saw the curious glances being shot at her as she hung onto Dylan's hand as they got him settled. Fortunately, nobody suggested that she should leave because there was no question of that happening. She intended to stay with him until he woke up…

If he woke up, a small voice whispered insidiously, but she closed her mind to that terrible thought. Dylan had to get better. He just had to for her sake and for the sake of their child!

She leant over the bed and kissed him gently on the lips, oblivious to the people who were watching. 'I love you, Dylan, and you have to get better for my sake and for our baby. We need you too much to lose you now.'

His head was thumping!

Dylan groaned as he tried to blot out the pain but it wouldn't go away. He knew he was in bed but couldn't understand why he felt so dreadful. His mind whirled as he struggled to remember what he'd been doing but everything was blank…everything apart from the voice that had kept whispering 'I love you' all through his dreams. He sighed because it was wishful thinking to hope that Joanna would tell him that when he woke up.

'Dylan, can you hear me, darling? I hope you can. I want you to know how much I love you and need you. I'm sorry that I've been so stupid but I was scared, you see, afraid that you might stop loving me and come to resent our baby.'

The voice came again, seeping into his consciousness once more, and he sighed because it was so wonderful to imagine Joanna saying those things to him. He loved her so much and all he wanted to do was tell her that.

So what was stopping him?

'I love you, too.'

His voice sounded like rusty nails being rattled around inside a tin bucket and he blinked in surprise then blinked again because he'd got the distinct impression the first time that there was someone bending over him.

'Dylan? Can you say that again?'

The excitement in Joanna's voice made him smile. If this *was* a dream it was a particularly good one so he may as well make the most of it while he could.

'I love you,' he repeated obligingly, rusty nails notwithstanding.

Pandemonium seemed to break out after that. Dylan was aware of several different voices all talking at once and groaned in dismay. There was only one voice he wanted to hear and that was Joanna's. Where was she? Had she gone away and left him?

His eyes slowly opened and he stared in bemusement at the crowd of people clustered around him. 'What's going on?' he croaked, desperately searching for that one special face. 'Where's Joanna?'

'I'm right here, darling.'

Suddenly she was there beside him, bending down to kiss him on the mouth so that he could taste the salty flavour of her tears on his lips. He tried to lift up his hand to touch her but he seemed to be tethered into place and couldn't move.

'Keep still, darling, or you'll dislodge the drip.'

'Drip?' he repeated, turning so he could look at his left arm. A flurry of shock skittered through him when he saw the plastic tubing that snaked up from his arm into a bag of fluid. He was about to ask what it was for when Joanna spoke to him again and he turned to her once more, thinking to himself that he could happily spend the rest of his life just lying here and looking at her beautiful face.

'You have no idea how wonderful it is to see you awake at last.' She smiled at him and his heart suddenly kicked up such a storm when he saw the expression in her eyes that the monitor alarm sounded.

Joanna laughed as she quickly reset the button. 'I hope that means what I think it does! But just so there is no misunderstanding I want you to know that I love you, Dylan. I've been waiting for you to wake up so I could tell you that.'

'I love you, too,' he murmured, struggling to take it all in. Joanna loved him and even though that was the most important thing of all he realised that he needed to know what was going on.

'I'm sorry, but I've no idea what's happened. Why have I got this drip in my arm and what did you mean about you waiting for me to wake up?'

'You're in the IC unit,' she explained gently. 'You've been here for three days.'

'The IC unit,' he repeated uncertainly. 'Have I been ill?'

'In a way, yes.'

She sounded concerned now and Dylan knew that it was because he couldn't remember what had happened. He struggled to force back the layers of fog in his mind and gasped when everything came rushing back.

'I was shot! I was in A and E, checking on a patient, when this guy came racing in, waving a gun.'

'That's right. The security staff tried to stop him and the gun went off. You were hit in the chest by a bullet and Diane had to operate on you.'

He heard the wobble in her voice and longed to hold

her in his arms and reassure her that he was fine, only he wasn't sure how he felt. 'And I've been here ever since?' he asked instead, not wanting to run before he could walk, so to speak.

'Yes.'

Dylan frowned because he sensed there was a lot more to the tale than she was admitting. However, before he had a chance to ask her anything else Martin Henshall, the IC consultant, appeared.

'So our star patient has decided to rejoin us, has he?' Martin observed cheerfully, taking the chart off one of the nurses who were crowded around the bed. 'Nice to have you back with us, Dylan. It might mean that the staff will pay attention to some of our other patients instead of spending all their time lavishing you with TLC.'

Martin chuckled when the staff groaned. 'Anyhow, I'll give you the once over just to check that everything is as it should be. Why don't you take a break now, Joanna, and come back in half an hour or so?'

'Don't be silly, Martin,' Joanna protested. 'I know exactly what needs doing so there's no reason for me to leave.'

'Even so, I'm sure Dylan would prefer it if you gave us a few minutes on our own.' Martin winked at him. 'There's nothing very romantic about having a catheter removed and I don't want him suing me because I've ruined his image.'

'Oh!' Joanna flushed as she quickly stood up. 'I'll be in my office so could you phone me when you've finished?'

'It would be far better if you went and had a cup of coffee instead of worrying about work,' Martin said firmly. He turned to Dylan and sighed. 'She's not left your side since you were admitted, so can you try and make her see sense?'

'You've been here all that time?' Dylan asked in amazement.

'Of course,' she responded tartly, but he could see the way she quickly averted her eyes. Even though she had told him quite openly and in front of everyone that she loved him, she was still rather shy about what had happened. His heart overflowed with tenderness as he captured her hand and gave her a gentle tug so that she had to bend over the bed.

'Go and take a break, Joanna,' he said softly so that only she could hear. 'If not for your sake then for the sake of our baby.'

Her eyes darkened with surprise. 'You could hear me when you were unconscious?'

'Yes. It's what made me fight to get better.' He let go of her hand and touched her cheek. 'I love you too much to ever leave you, my darling.'

Tears welled to her eyes but she blinked them away as she smiled at him—the most glorious smile he had ever seen on anyone's face. She kissed him full on the mouth then laughed when the staff broke out into a spontaneous round of applause.

'And now I think I'd better make a speedy exit before we cause any more chaos,' she declared, stepping back from the bed. She waggled her fingers at him then hurried away.

Dylan smiled as Martin set about making sure he was on the mend, unprotesting as he suffered the usual indignities of the sick. What did it matter if he was being prodded and poked and checked in parts of his anatomy that he would normally keep well covered?

Joanna loved him and he would walk naked through the streets of London if she asked him to!

Finally all the checks were done and Martin left with instructions that he should rest, not that he'd needed to tell him that. Dylan sighed as his eyes began to close of their own accord. He desperately wanted to stay awake until Joanna came back but he was exhausted. Still, she would be here when he woke up.

His heart lifted with joy. She would *always* be here for him from now on, just as he would always be there for her. On that happy thought he drifted off to sleep and dreamed of Joanna and their baby and the wonderful times they would have together. And the best thing of all was that the dream would continue when he woke up.

'Are you sure I look all right? I mean, my bump is really starting to show now…'

'You look wonderful! You look exactly like a woman who is almost four months pregnant should look.'

Joanna laughed when Dylan took her into his arms and kissed her. 'You can be very convincing, especially when you do that!'

'Good. It's nice to know that I achieve positive results.' He kissed her again then sighed with pleasure. 'I didn't believe life could ever be this good.'

'I know what you mean,' she agreed, nestling into his arms and thinking about what had happened in the past few weeks.

Once Dylan had been discharged from hospital he had moved into her flat. It had been pointless him going back home when they wanted to be together so much. Joanna had taken a long-overdue holiday and had spent the time making sure that he didn't do too much while his injuries had healed. There was still some residual stiffness in the joint but physiotherapy should cure that eventually. He was hoping to return to work soon but in the meantime they were making the most of their time together.

Despite all her fears, everyone had been wonderfully supportive. They'd received lots of cards and messages of congratulation when it had become known they were expecting a baby. Joanna had been deeply touched when Brian Maxwell had informed her that the hospital trust was willing to to let her work part time after she'd had the baby. It was an option she was considering although she wouldn't make her final decision until after she finished her maternity leave. Now, however, they were going to visit Dylan's parents and tell them about the baby, hence her desire to look her best.

She stepped out of his arms and went to stand in front of the mirror, turning sideways so she could study the swell of her stomach. Her figure had changed in other ways as well and the new fullness of her breasts was clearly visible. The baby was growing fast and they'd both been thrilled when they'd been told after a recent scan that it was a little boy. She was carrying Dylan's son and the pleasure that thought gave her was hard to describe.

'It's just so fantastic, isn't it?' He came and put his arms around her, letting his hands rest on the bump. 'Just think, you've got our son in there and he's getting bigger every day.'

'I know. It's such an amazing feeling. I can't really describe how it makes me feel,' she admitted.

'So you're not sorry that you decided to keep him?'

he asked softly, nuzzling her neck with his lips and making her shiver.

'No. I never wanted to have a termination and only considered it because it seemed the best thing to do in the circumstances.' There was a catch in her voice when she realised what a mistake it would have been and how much she would have regretted it.

Dylan obviously understood because he turned her to face him. 'But everything turned out all right in the end, didn't it? Maybe I should be grateful to that chap for shooting me because otherwise we might not have reached this point.'

'I don't know about that,' she said with a shudder, then sighed. 'I was so mixed up at the time that I can't swear I wouldn't have told you how much I loved you eventually, but I *feel* it in here.' She placed her hand on her heart as she looked at him. 'Does that make sense?'

'Perfect sense. And I know how hard it was for you to reach a decision because you'd always kept your emotions buried until we met.'

'That's true. I suppose I was afraid of letting myself fall in love in case I got hurt,' she admitted, wondering why it had taken her so long to understand that. She smiled as she reached up and kissed him lightly on the mouth. 'I just needed to find the right person, the one I could trust, before I could let myself go.'

'Thank heavens that person was me!' he replied, grinning at her. He suddenly sobered. 'Now, there's one more question I want to ask you before we set off.'

'That sounds very serious,' she teased.

'It is. It's the most important question I have ever asked in the whole of my life.' He took a deep breath.

'Will you marry me, Joanna? I know it's not the fashionable thing to do in this day and age but there is nothing I want more than to know that you are my wife. I also want this child we're having to enjoy the stability that comes from having parents who have committed themselves to one another in the eyes of God and the law. Does that sound ridiculously antiquated to you?'

'No, it doesn't. It sounds right because it's what I want as well.' She slid her arms around his waist and hugged him. 'I want to make that kind of a commitment to you, Dylan, and not just for the baby's sake but because I want the security of knowing that we shall always belong together.'

'Then let's not wait. Let's set a date just as soon as we can.' He bent and kissed her, and she was touched when she saw that his eyes were filled with tears.

'I love you, Joanna Martin.'

'And I love you, Dylan Archer.' She stopped and frowned then nodded happily. 'Joanna Archer. Mmm, I like it. It has a certain ring to it, wouldn't you agree?'

'Yes,' he growled, then kissed her again—at which point the conversation ended. Joanna kissed him back, thinking that they were going to be very, very late by the time they made it to his parents' house!

Five months later...

Little Michael James Archer arrived in the world at ten minutes before midnight and was immediately placed into his father's arms. Dylan brushed a kiss against his son's sticky little head, wondering if life could get any better than this. He carried the baby to the bed and bent to kiss Joanna. 'Thank you, darling. Thank you so much.'

'He's gorgeous, isn't he?'

The wonderment in her voice as he placed the baby in her arms brought a lump to his throat. It had been a hard labour and she must be exhausted, but there was no doubting her joy at the safe delivery of their son.

'He is.' Dylan smiled when she glanced at him. 'I'm a bit overcome by it all, I'm afraid.'

'Me, too,' she whispered, pulling him down onto the bed beside her. She kissed him on the cheek then took his hand and gently placed it on the baby's head. 'Feel him, Dylan. He's the living, breathing proof of our love and that makes him the most special child in the whole wide world, doesn't it?'

'Yes. He's very special. And you're very special, too, Joanna.'

He bent and kissed her, kissed her a second time and then a third because this was the most magical moment of his life. He had his wife and his child right here and there was nothing more he could ever want out of life. And the best thing of all was knowing that Joanna felt the same way he did!

Modern Romance™
...seduction and
passion guaranteed

Tender Romance™
...love affairs that
last a lifetime

Medical Romance™
...medical drama
on the pulse

Historical Romance™
...rich, vivid and
passionate

Sensual Romance™
...sassy, sexy and
seductive

Blaze Romance™
...the temperature's
rising

27 new titles every month.

Live the emotion

MILLS & BOON®

MB3

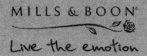

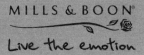

MILLS & BOON®

Live the emotion

Medical Romance™

THE DOCTOR'S FAMILY SECRET by *Joanna Neil*

When new A&E consultant Nick Hilliard sweeps in, full of ideas for change, Dr Laura Brett is torn between her attraction for this man and her concern for the department. But Nick becomes a rock for Laura – his support is unconditional. And then his ambitious plans start to affect her father, and her loyalties are divided...

A SURGEON FOR KATE by *Janet Ferguson*

Surgeon Lucas Brown may be the heart-throb of Seftonbridge General, but nurse Kate Maybury is staying well clear. A new relationship is the last thing on her agenda. But the sexual tension is crackling between them, and Kate knows she faces a struggle to hold on to her heart...

THE CONSULTANT'S TEMPTATION
by *Emily Forbes*

Gorgeous consultant Will MacLeod couldn't believe his luck when his new registrar, Alice Ferguson, turned out to be talented *and* beautiful. But he refused to endanger her promising career by indulging their chemistry. However, Alice was not going to let Will's scruples stand in the way of the love of a lifetime.

On sale 6th February 2004

Available at most branches of WHSmith, Tesco, Martins, Borders, Eason, Sainsbury's and all good paperback bookshops.

Behind the Red Doors

Sassy, sensual...and provocatively playful!

Vicki Lewis Thompson

Stephanie Bond

Leslie Kelly

On sale 6th February 2004

Available at most branches of WHSmith, Tesco, Martins, Borders, Eason, Sainsbury's and all good paperback bookshops.

4 FREE

books and a surprise gift!

We would like to take this opportunity to thank you for reading this Mills & Boon® book by offering you the chance to take FOUR more specially selected titles from the Medical Romance™ series absolutely FREE! We're also making this offer to introduce you to the benefits of the Reader Service™—

- ★ FREE home delivery
- ★ FREE gifts and competitions
- ★ FREE monthly Newsletter
- ★ Exclusive Reader Service offers
- ★ Books available before they're in the shops

Accepting these FREE books and gift places you under no obligation to buy, you may cancel at any time, even after receiving your free shipment. Simply complete your details below and return the entire page to the address below. *You don't even need a stamp!*

YES! Please send me 4 free Medical Romance books and a surprise gift. I understand that unless you hear from me, I will receive 6 superb new titles every month for just £2.60 each, postage and packing free. I am under no obligation to purchase any books and may cancel my subscription at any time. The free books and gift will be mine to keep in any case.

M4ZED

Ms/Mrs/Miss/Mr ....Initials...................................
BLOCK CAPITALS PLEASE

Surname ....

Address ....

....

....Postcode...............................

Send this whole page to:
UK: FREEPOST CN81, Croydon, CR9 3WZ
EIRE: PO Box 4546, Kilcock, County Kildare (stamp required)